THE HARDER WE FALL

A SWEETGUM MEADOWS ROMANCE BOOK 9

IMANI PRICE

First Edition: March 2025

ISBN 978-1-960207-64-7 (ebook)
ISBN 978-1-960207-65-4 (paperback)

Published by Books to Hook Publishing, LLC.
www.BooksToHook.com

CONTENTS

CHAPTER ONE

Aimee cradled the last neatly folded tortilla in her hand, pausing to inhale the comforting aroma of slow-roasted chicken mingling with creamy dressing. Each wrap felt like a miniature masterpiece—proof of the care she poured into her cooking. Across her small kitchen, an ambitious spread of ingredients covered nearly every inch of counter space: fresh bell peppers, crisp lettuce, homemade sauces, and the leftover chicken filling that teased her senses with a smoky, seasoned fragrance.

She counted the rows of finished wraps for the third time, murmuring under her breath, "Six... seven... eight." A satisfied smile slipped across her face. *All there.* The soft hum of her overhead light buzzed in harmony with her own excitement, even as her feet throbbed from standing all morning. Every dish was a promise to make tonight's celebration special.

"Finally," she whispered, placing the final wrap into a snug row in her large aluminum tray. The pride in her voice was a gentle reward for the hours spent chopping, stirring, and tasting until the flavors sang in perfect harmony.

Her tiny kitchen felt steamy, scented with garlic and herbs—

if she closed her eyes, she could almost imagine she was standing in a bustling restaurant kitchen instead of her cozy, one-bedroom home. *At least no one's here to see this mess,* she thought wryly, eyeing the precarious tower of mixing bowls and pans balanced by the sink. She would deal with them eventually, but first, she had an engagement party to set up—and she refused to keep her best friend Maia waiting on her own big night.

A shrill ring pierced the air, snapping her from her momentary daydream. Aimee wiped her hands on the nearest towel, hurrying into the living room. Dust motes twirled in the sunbeam spilling through the window, and the phone on her TV stand wouldn't let up with its insistent *briiing-briiing.*

She picked up the receiver. "Hello?"

"Aimee!" Maia's voice chimed through with familiar warmth. "How's the cooking going? You hanging in there?"

Instantly, Aimee's shoulders relaxed; it helped that this voice belonged to the very friend she was cooking for. "Not gonna lie, I'm knee-deep in bowls, but I'm alive," she joked, stepping around a box of extra utensils she'd dragged in last night. "You know me—I'd do anything for you, even take on an army of dishes."

A delighted laugh answered her. "And that's exactly why you're my best friend. Seriously, though, I can't thank you enough. You're basically catering my entire engagement party. You sure you're not exhausted?"

Aimee tossed a glance at the mountain of dishes. *Exhausted,* she might be, but she refused to let that overshadow her excitement. "Maybe a little," she admitted, tone still light. "But for you? Worth it. What's a few calluses compared to a friend's big day?"

She heard Maia sigh with relief. "I still owe you a million times over for this. Anyway, I just wanted to remind you to pick up the ice cream cake from Scoop There It Is before heading over. It's the one dessert I knew I couldn't trust myself to make or transport."

Aimee mentally scrolled through the day's to-do list, ensuring she hadn't forgotten anything. "Yup, it's on my radar. I'll swing by in—" she peeked at the clock—"thirty minutes or so. That'll put me at the Community Center with enough time to set up the buffet table."

Maia's joyful giggle sent a spark of warmth through the line. "I could hug you right now. Can't wait to see everything. I'm already imagining your famous wraps, the mac n' cheese, and... oh, the fish balls you hinted at!"

"Patience," Aimee teased, though Maia's excitement was contagious. "You'll taste it all soon enough. Now let me handle this final prep. Go on and enjoy being the bride-to-be, Ms. Future Mrs. Zhang."

A playful squeal echoed. "I still can't believe I'm getting a second shot at real love," Maia said, her voice more serious for an instant. "Thank you for making it extra memorable."

With a gentle smile, Aimee pressed the phone to her ear. "That's what friends are for. Now shoo—let me finish or I'll be late."

"All right, all right. Love you, bestie."

"Love you, too," Aimee whispered, and the call ended with a soft click.

Setting the phone down, she savored the moment's quiet. Through her living room window, her sleepy residential street stretched out, each house and building wearing a welcoming, timeworn charm. She inhaled a lungful of warm afternoon air, balancing that sense of calm against the thrill fluttering in her chest. In no time, her best friend would be surrounded by family and friends, celebrating the kind of second chance some people only dream about. *And I get to be a part of it.*

Turning on her heel, Aimee marched back into the kitchen, determined to wrap up the last details. Though exhaustion tugged at her limbs, there was a brightness in her soul that kept her moving. After all, this was for Maia.

EXACTLY THIRTY-FIVE MINUTES LATER, Aimee parked her old green minivan in front of Scoop There It Is, the local ice cream parlor. Evening sunlight illuminated the swirling pink-and-white awning, making it look deliciously whimsical. She tugged her scarf tighter around her neck, stepping out into a mellow autumn breeze that carried the scent of caramel from the bakery next door.

Ding-a-ling. The door's bell announced her arrival, and she was promptly greeted by the sweet chill of the shop's interior. Rows of pastel chairs lined the walls, and a giant chalkboard menu proudly flaunted flavors like "Peachy Keen" and "Chocolate Coma." Aimee's stomach rumbled at the sugary perfume of waffle cones, but she reminded herself there was no time for sampling.

"Hey!" called India, a petite woman wearing a bright pink apron stretched over the slightest hint of a baby bump. "You're here for the engagement cake, right?"

"That's me," Aimee affirmed, stepping closer to the counter. While India disappeared into the back, Aimee took a moment to drink in the cheerful surroundings: colorful murals of dancing ice cream scoops, a shelf stacked with sprinkles in more flavors than she even knew existed. A memory tugged at her—Maia, months ago, promising they'd throw themselves "big girl parties" with sundaes if real life ever got too stressful.

We've come such a long way, Aimee thought with fondness.

A moment later, India reemerged with a large, decorative box that exuded frosty air. "Careful," she warned, placing it gently on the counter. "Rashad put extra dry ice in there so it stays firm longer."

"Thank you so much," Aimee said, carefully sliding the box into her arms. The cold seeped through her sleeves. "Between your cake and my homemade food, I'm pretty sure we're about to spoil everyone tonight."

India's face glowed with shared excitement. "You tell Maia I said congratulations," she said. Then, more quietly, she patted her belly. "Babies and weddings... seems like good news is everywhere these days, huh?"

Aimee's heart pinched at that hopeful statement. She forced a bright smile. "Definitely. Good news is something we could all use more of."

Stepping out into the golden hour light, she settled the box securely in the passenger seat of her van. *Onward,* she thought. *No time to daydream.* The sky's cotton-candy pink hints dissolved into warm orange as she navigated the gentle streets of Sweetgum, crossing the railroad tracks that led toward the Community Center. Each block passed in a blur of old brick storefronts and vintage lampposts, exuding that cozy small-town spirit she'd grown to love.

By the time Aimee parked at the Community Center, her breath was coming in small puffs, more from excitement than strain. The brick building—adorned with twinkling string lights for the party—gave off a friendly glow in the early twilight. A couple of Maia's friends, Serena and Joy, rushed over the moment they spotted Aimee's van rattling up.

"There you are!" Serena exclaimed, reaching for the trays of food from the back seat. The waft of savory herbs escaped the foil-covered pans, making her eyes gleam. "We've got a long table set up inside, just like you asked."

Aimee hopped out and carefully lifted the precious ice cream cake box. "Thanks, you two. If you can help me get the trays in,

I'll handle the cake. Let's do this quickly—it's safer in the cooler."

Within minutes, they were ducking through the tall double doors into the wide-open event hall. Pale fairy lights looped around the perimeter, shimmering against white tablecloths. The hum of cheerful conversation, along with the echo of footsteps on polished floors, created a bright, welcoming backdrop.

Aimee's gaze flicked straight to Maia—standing near a gleaming backdrop of pastel balloons, she looked luminous in a fitted ivory dress. Her dark hair was swept into a loose updo, a few curls framing her cheeks. The man by her side, Alex, was impeccably dressed but noticeably starry-eyed whenever he glanced at his fiancée.

A love that was nearly lost to heartbreak before, Aimee recalled, remembering how Maia's first marriage had crumbled. *And yet here she is, absolutely glowing.* Pride warmed Aimee's chest.

"Girl, you made it!" Maia beamed and strode forward, hands already reaching to help with the boxes, although she was the *last* person who should be lugging trays around at her own engagement party.

Aimee angled her hip to block Maia's attempt. "Nope, not tonight. You focus on playing the radiant bride-to-be."

Maia rolled her eyes but grinned, hooking an arm around Aimee's waist for a quick hug. "You look exhausted. But you're my hero. Thank you for doing all this."

A fresh wave of gratitude and affection pulsed through Aimee. "Your happiness is worth it. And trust me, seeing you two about to start a new chapter is a boost by itself." She gently nudged Maia toward Alex, who shot them a friendly wave.

They moved to the long buffet table near the front of the hall. The overhead lights revealed pink linens and neat centerpieces of fresh roses and baby's breath—Maia's favorite. A sweet, mild fragrance of flowers mingled with the comforting scent of Aimee's cooking, creating a cocoon of warmth within the lively space.

Maia peeked under the foil of one tray. "Oh my goodness, the fish balls smell amazing!" She popped one into her mouth, nodding rapidly. "Unreal. Everyone is going to flip."

Aimee stifled a laugh. "I hope so. You know I'm always my toughest critic in the kitchen."

Behind them, a lively chorus of greetings swelled: college friends squealing and hugging, older relatives laughing while investigating the drink station, a group of neighbors snapping selfies by the balloon arch. The chatter vibrated with excitement for the soon-to-be-weds.

Shifting the last tray into place, Aimee sighed in relief. Her entire body ached from the day's marathon cooking session, yet a joyous buzz coursed through her veins. She stole a glance at Maia, who now stood by Alex accepting congratulations. Their hands were linked, fingers interlaced—two separate worlds fused into one. Aimee's heart squeezed. *They really are perfect together.*

Then she remembered the ice cream cake. *Focus,* she chided herself. *It's still in the cooler.* While everyone chatted, Aimee discreetly made her way to the kitchen behind the stage area. The small fridge she'd requested was plugged in, humming softly. Carefully, she tucked the dessert inside, ensuring it would remain solid until the grand reveal.

Turning to head back out, she paused at the threshold. A wide window offered a glimpse of the hall. The dance floor sat empty for the moment, though a DJ tested a track in the corner, the bass line thumping faintly through the speakers. A swirl of anticipation fluttered in Aimee's stomach—this was more than a gathering; it was a celebration of fresh love, second chances, and the belief that hope could bloom again in the same place heartbreak once took root.

Smoothing her sweater, she sucked in a breath and stepped out into the hall. *Don't go getting sentimental—there's work to do.*

~

WITH THE BUFFET ready and the guests beginning to indulge in her carefully crafted dishes, Aimee finally grabbed herself a small plate. She picked up a dainty sample of the homemade fish balls, plus half a wrap, letting the savory tang burst across her tongue. A faint *mmm* escaped her lips. Satisfying, though she could still taste every moment of her own labor in the marinade.

"Where's that unstoppable chef?" came a jovial voice from behind.

Aimee turned, meeting Garrett's playful gaze. Tall and fashionable, he sported a stylishly tailored suit that shouted big-city flair rather than small-town vibes. "We need to talk about your mind-blowing mac n' cheese," he teased, giving her a little bow. "I almost cried at the taste."

Her cheeks warmed. "You're being dramatic."

"Trust me," Garrett countered, pressing a hand to his chest, "I've eaten my way through countless events, but yours? Practically an emotional journey." He angled his head. "Don't hide behind that modesty. Own your brilliance."

A ripple of self-conscious pride fluttered through her. "Thank you," she managed, smiling at his effusive praise. In truth, cooking had always felt more like second nature than a showy skill. But hearing such compliments, especially tonight, reminded her that maybe her efforts had real value outside her own kitchen.

"Later," Garrett went on, "you have to share your secret. I won't rest until I uncover the hidden ingredient in that cheese sauce."

She tilted her head with a mischievous grin. "Garrett, if I told you, it wouldn't be a secret anymore."

He pressed a theatrical hand to his heart. "You wound me. All right, I see how it is. Keep your culinary brilliance locked away."

Laughing, Aimee shooed him toward the dance floor where the DJ had switched to a slow groove, inviting the first wave of dancers. Sparks of pink and gold from the overhead disco ball glittered across the floor.

Standing momentarily alone, Aimee glanced around at all the smiling faces, the high spirits, the swirl of celebratory attire. *When was the last time she felt this rush of excitement for herself?* She and Maia had grown up making fantasies about their futures: they'd plan big weddings, help raise each other's kids, and host backyard barbecues every summer. Maia was now halfway through that dream, while Aimee... She let out a small sigh. Four heartbreaks in a year was enough to dampen anyone's faith. Maybe love would come in its own time. For now, she was content to witness Maia's joy.

"Penny for your thoughts," Maia's voice chimed, drawing her out of her reverie. They found themselves side by side again, away from the crowd.

"Oh, just thinking about how perfect everything looks," Aimee lied smoothly, eyes drifting toward the pastel streamers overhead.

"And thinking about how you're always the one making everyone else's party happen, but never your own?" Maia guessed gently, following Aimee's gaze.

Heat crept up Aimee's cheeks. *She knows me too well.* "Maia, stop reading my mind. It's embarrassing."

"Don't be embarrassed. I get it," Maia said, looping an arm through Aimee's. Her voice turned quiet with compassion. "It's okay to want a piece of this kind of happiness for yourself, you know."

"I never said I didn't want it," Aimee murmured, her eyes fixed on a swirl of confetti that drifted across the floor. She drew in a breath, letting the swirl of love and laughter in the air fill her lungs. "But I'm not in a rush. Not anymore."

Maia pressed a light squeeze to Aimee's arm. "Just promise me you won't shut the door on possibilities. Sometimes love sneaks in through unexpected windows."

A tiny pang echoed in Aimee's chest as she remembered her grandmother's old saying about life's many doors and windows. "I'll try," she conceded.

The music shifted to a mid-tempo track, and a wave of guests eagerly filled the dance floor. Maia's face lit up. "Come on," she said, giving Aimee a playful tug. "We should at least do one quick dance before everyone claims you for more cooking advice."

Protests hovered on Aimee's lips—her feet ached, she was sweaty from the kitchen, and the swirl of the party felt nearly overwhelming. But seeing Maia's excitement made it impossible to refuse. "Okay, just one," she relented, letting her friend tug her toward the throng of dancers.

The next few minutes blurred into a spirited swirl of music, laughter, and the muffled stomps of feet on the polished floor. Aimee twirled, letting the steady beat carry her exhaustion away. Every so often, the crowd parted enough for her to glimpse Maia and Alex dancing together. The awe in his expression was genuine, a man smitten with the woman in his arms. Another wave of longing pulsed through Aimee, a delicate ache she tried to smother. *They deserve that happiness. I'm just glad to stand here and see it.*

When the song ended, the DJ launched into a livelier track, and the crowd's energy morphed into a playful frenzy. Aimee excused herself with a wide grin, weaving through the dancers to snag a bottle of water from the refreshment table. She caught her breath and gently pressed a hand to her abdomen, trying to soothe the flutter of mingled joy and wistfulness.

Garrett shouted a cheerful farewell from across the room; he was bounding off to lead a conga line that was spontaneously forming. Maia and Alex were pulled into the parade, their laughter ringing out above the music. Watching from the sidelines, Aimee chuckled.

And that was when she realized: *she truly felt content.* A surprising pocket of peace settled inside her chest. For tonight, everything was as it should be—Maia celebrating a second chance at love, Aimee quietly witnessing the fruits of her own labor in the form of grinning, well-fed guests.

By the end of the evening, when she helped cut the ice cream cake—perfectly decorated with delicate sugar flowers—and served slices to a chorus of delighted cheers, Aimee felt like her heart might burst from fullness. *This* was the payoff of every sore muscle and frazzled morning in the kitchen: a community of friends bonding over shared food and genuine affection.

Long after the last slice of cake was devoured and the final fish ball vanished, Aimee found herself gathering empty trays and leftover sauces. The hall's overhead lights brightened, signaling the official wind-down. Maia and Alex stood at the door, hugging guests goodnight, still floating on the promise of their soon-to-be vows.

Deep breath, Aimee told herself, sliding the final tray into her carrying case. Her limbs felt like lead, yet her spirit glowed with the knowledge of a job well done. Humming softly, she hauled the trays toward the exit, the quiet chatter of straggling guests echoing off the high ceilings.

She paused once at the threshold, glancing back at the decorated hall. Streamers drooped, confetti littered the floor, and the fairy lights glistened overhead. Memories of the laughter, dancing, and those sparks of soon-to-be wedded bliss flooded her anew. She pressed a hand to her heart. "Good night, party," she whispered, a slight hitch in her voice.

Turning on her heel, Aimee pushed out into the balmy night air. The hush of Sweetgum's sleepy streets caressed her ears after the evening's whirlwind. Moonlight caught the soft angles of the town's skyline, every storefront dimmed for the night. She felt cocooned by a sense of hope clinging to the edges of this peaceful darkness.

One day, maybe, her heart whispered before her mind could stop it. *One day, maybe that kind of love will find me, too.*

But for now, with the hush of midnight approaching, she could let her happiness be about Maia. And that was perfectly, beautifully enough.

CHAPTER TWO

Sweetgum felt different in the fall, and that difference seeped into Malakai's bones the moment he stepped onto its sidewalks. The air lacked the thick humidity he remembered from countless summers here—those sweltering Julys that made every breath feel like sipping hot soup. Now, with September half gone, the breeze rolling down Main Street held a gentle coolness. Everywhere he looked, leaves dipped from vibrant green into soft gold, each tree poised to burst into full autumn glory.

He took a slow breath, letting the crisp air refresh his lungs. *New season, new start.* The phrase tugged at him, echoing his own reinvention. He'd returned to Sweetgum an older, more deliberate man than the restless teen who left so many summers ago. Back then, the town's rhythms had felt too small, too confining. Now, after years away, the quiet charm was precisely what he craved.

Outside his modest apartment building, he fiddled with a small ceramic teapot—a goofy souvenir he'd picked up earlier in the day. He stared at the handcrafted swirls of paint, vivid blues and greens that sparked a sense of whimsy. Carefully, he positioned it on his TV stand, stepping back as though he were curating a gallery piece.

"There," he murmured, squinting to appreciate the pop of color against the neutral space. The teapot radiated a playful energy that gently broke up the plain beige walls. *A small token to say this is my place now.*

Surveying the apartment, Malakai exhaled a blend of satisfaction and relief. He'd spent the past few days making this rented space feel like home—placing vases, hanging curtains, folding clothes into dressers. It was cozy and unassuming, sure, but something about *cozy* finally appealed to him. After a life of shifting among big-city apartments and cold university dorms, he wanted warmth. He wanted *home.*

He sank into the couch, resting his head on the cushions. His mind still buzzed with mental checklists of everything left to do—furniture to assemble, the final touches on the living room décor. But for tonight, he had another mission: meet with Aunt Rochelle at her diner. She'd closed up early just so they could talk privately about her future—and, by extension, his.

A quick glance at his watch told him it was already eight o'clock. Perfect timing. Rolling his shoulders to chase away tension, Malakai stood and headed to the bathroom to splash cool water on his face. The small hallway creaked underfoot, carrying him past framed photos of family he'd lost and family he still clung to—most of all, Aunt Rochelle.

Focus, he reminded himself. He brushed down the edges of his short beard, then shrugged on a light jacket. The soft hum of the night air reached him as he slipped outside, locking the door behind him. The lampposts along the sidewalk glowed like gentle beacons, guiding him toward the heart of Sweetgum. He felt an odd, buoyant excitement ripple through his chest. Returning here no longer felt like an obligation. It felt like a fresh chapter, beckoning him to turn the page.

BY THE TIME Malakai stepped into Rochelle's Old-Fashioned Diner, a hush had settled over the place. A warm glow from the overhead lights revealed just a smattering of customers lingering over late-night coffee. The scent of fried onions and homemade pies kissed the air, reminding him of childhood summers when he'd perch on a stool and watch Aunt Rochelle serve plate after plate with her characteristic flair.

He hovered near the entrance for a moment, soaking it in—laminated menus fanned out on the counter, the dull gleam of a jukebox in the corner, small vases with plastic daisies brightening each table. *Some things never change,* he thought with a nostalgic ache. *And thank God for that.*

Aunt Rochelle spotted him instantly. Though her face carried more lines than he remembered, her grin was as wide and radiant as ever. "There's my boy," she announced, waving him in. Even from behind the counter, her presence filled the room, her apron tied expertly around her waist, hair in a neat wrap under a hairnet. "You'd best get over here before I eat this last slice of pie myself."

Malakai smiled, crossing the checkerboard floor. He slid onto the stool in front of her, noticing she'd already prepared a plate of peach pie crowned with a swirl of whipped cream. "You spoil me," he teased, picking up the fork. "So, how's it been today?"

She exhaled, making a face that hinted at both pride and fatigue. "Busy enough that my feet are threatening to leave me," she said with a wry smile. "We hosted a baby shower earlier. Confetti everywhere. Kids running around like they owned the place. You'd have loved it."

He savored a bite of the pie, feeling the buttery crust melt on his tongue. "Hmm," he hummed, eyes drifting closed in enjoyment. "This is exactly what I needed." The sweetness danced over his taste buds, reminding him again of his childhood visits. He'd once believed no pie could surpass Aunt Rochelle's, and so far, that remained true.

Aunt Rochelle propped an elbow on the counter, rubbing her shoulder with her free hand. "Maybe, but it sure has me beat. So," she said, adjusting her stance, "is Sweetgum boring you yet? After all that fancy traveling you did, coming back here might feel like stepping into slow motion."

Malakai let out a low chuckle, swirling his fork thoughtfully in the leftover crumbs. "Not at all," he answered, glancing around at the peaceful diner. "I think I've grown up enough to appreciate slow motion."

Her lips curved into a satisfied smile, though she tried to hide it behind mild skepticism. "Well, look at you, sounding all wise. City Boy has matured." Then, softening, she eyed his jacket. "But for real, baby, how's your day been? You settling in okay? Don't you go coddling that apartment too much. You need to meet people. Let Sweetgum remind you of all the good stuff you used to love."

He shrugged, taking another forkful of pie. "I did explore. Bought some stuff for decorating, actually." He laughed under his breath. "Little knickknacks here and there. Might've gotten carried away."

"Decorating, huh?" she echoed, studying him with a fond tilt of her head. "I knew you were serious about this move, but hearing you talk like that… it's nice, baby. Real nice. I just hope you're not planning to run off again in six months."

Malakai shook his head, letting the pie's warmth settle into his chest. "Not planning on it," he said softly. He could sense how much that answer mattered to her. After his parents' deaths, Aunt Rochelle had become his anchor—but he'd slipped free too often, chasing one ambition after another. "I want to be here for you, Aunt Rochelle. That's why I came back."

She reached out and patted his hand, her gaze brimming

with a mixture of pride and relief. "Well, I'm glad." Then she winced, rotating her shoulder gingerly. "I don't know how many more long shifts these old bones can handle. I've been running this diner half my life, Malakai. Getting to the point where I need backup—real backup."

He let her words settle in the space between them. The echo of the broom scraping near the back reminded him of the simple fact: she'd been working nonstop all day, and her staff was probably as tired as she was. Malakai straightened, the desire to protect and uplift her surging in his chest.

"Let me help," he said firmly, folding his arms on the counter. "I have a ton of ideas for expansions, marketing angles to bring in extra customers. It might mean stepping outside the comfort zone a bit—theme nights, new menu items—but it'll keep this place thriving. And you can finally catch a break."

Aunt Rochelle's brow quirked up. "You trying to turn my diner into some second-rate tourist trap?" Despite her playful tone, her eyes held a spark of genuine concern. "What about all my regulars?"

Malakai reached out to give her hand a reassuring squeeze. "We can keep things authentic, Auntie. I promise. This place is part of the town's identity—I'm not looking to uproot that. Just want to spice things up so you can make more money with fewer back-breaking hours."

She exhaled, easing off her throbbing shoulder. "Mmm-hmm." A pause. "All right, baby. I trust you." Then her voice dropped, a tired edge softening her words. "But I ain't some spring chicken. If we're doing this, let's do it soon. I'd like to step back before these bones give up entirely."

A gentle wave of affection spread through him. "That's the plan," he promised. "But before we jump in, there's one thing I want to try..." His lips tugged into a wry half-smile. "I guess you could call it *Operation Undercover Boss.*"

She blinked. "Huh?"

He lowered his voice, even though there were hardly any customers around to overhear. "If the staff knows who I really am, they might treat me differently, show me the rose-colored version of operations. I need to see the day-to-day raw reality so we know exactly what to improve."

Understanding flickered in her eyes. "So, you want to stroll in here like some random customer, watch us from the sidelines. Then, once you see what's what, you'll reveal yourself as the new management? That about right?"

Malakai tapped the side of his fork against the empty plate, a note of anticipation vibrating through him. "Exactly. I want to see where the diner shines and where it might need a little polish. But for it to work, you have to pretend you've never laid eyes on me. At least in front of the staff."

Aunt Rochelle's gaze swept across his features, reading his determination. Then she nodded, her lips curving into a knowing smile. "Well, that sure is a fancy plan. You might run into folks who remember you, but it has been ages. Lord knows half the town's memory gets fuzzy when it comes to who lived where and when."

He dipped his head in agreement, excitement jumping in his pulse. "Right. So, hopefully, I can blend in without raising suspicion. Just don't slip and call me by name, or go bragging that your nephew's back in town."

She snorted. "Please. I'm not some gossiping fool. I can keep a secret—just don't expect me to stifle my pride forever. I *am* proud of you, you know."

Warmth bubbled in his chest. He pushed the empty pie plate aside, leaning across the counter. "Thank you, Aunt Rochelle. Truly. This means a lot. I want to do right by you."

A shadow of emotion passed over her face—love, relief, and just a hint of sadness that time had robbed them of so many years. Then she patted his arm and offered a lopsided grin. "I know you will, baby. I know."

The scraping sound at the back of the diner finally ceased, replaced by the quiet clank of the broom. The older gentleman near the window slipped out, leaving them nearly alone. The overhead fluorescent lights hummed, making the space feel intimate, as though they were the only two people awake in the entire town.

She broke the hush with a teasing glint in her eye. "Now, if you're done with your fancy business talk, how 'bout you help an old lady feel better by letting her feed you another slice of that pie? Or do you want to pretend you've never tasted it before?"

A chuckle rumbled from Malakai's throat, the tension melting away. "I'm never one to turn down a second slice. Operation Undercover Boss starts *after* I've had my fill of Aunt Rochelle's pie."

She laughed, a short, warm sound that flooded him with nostalgia. As she bustled off to fetch more pie, he relaxed into the stool. *This is exactly where I need to be,* he told himself, and for once, he believed it fully.

Tonight, though the diner's lights flickered over empty tables, Malakai could sense the promise of what it could become —and the promise of a future for him in Sweetgum. With each sweet, creamy bite of pie, his conviction grew. He was home, back to nurture the woman who had nurtured him, and maybe —just maybe—discover a life richer than any city skyline could ever offer.

He watched Aunt Rochelle hum a tune while she cut the slice, the comforting notes weaving through the gentle clatter in the kitchen. *Yes,* he thought, shoulders easing into contentment. *It's good to be home.*

CHAPTER THREE

"*D*arn leaky coffee," Aimee muttered, glaring at the fresh brown ring seeping onto the countertop. The ancient brewer was set on giving her extra headaches today, but she had no time to argue with a machine—morning rush was at its peak. She flipped the final pancake onto a plate and slid it in front of Mr. James with a flourish.

"There you go," she announced, pride coloring her voice. "Six freshly made pancakes, full of love and sunshine."

Mr. James patted his ample belly. "Much appreciated, Ms. Aimee, but next time, don't skip the strawberry smiley face. It's half the fun."

She was about to retort when the jingling doorbell signaled *more* arrivals. "Morning, Mrs. Frank!" Aimee called, spotting the harried woman rushing in. "The usual?"

Mrs. Frank paused just long enough to confirm, "Yes, and add sausages. I'm late!"—then scurried between booths, looking for an unclaimed seat.

Aimee smothered a laugh. Mondays were always wild, but her buoyant mood from Saturday's engagement party still lingered. Maia's excited calls over the weekend had made even her 4 a.m. wake-up feel like a pleasant dream. *Nothing's going to spoil this energy,* she decided, wiping a tiny bead of sweat from her brow.

"Ah, Ms. Aimee," Mr. James chimed in around a mouthful of pancake. "You did skip my strawberry garnish."

"You said you were in a hurry," she teased, reaching for a fresh pot of coffee. She poured it carefully into a customer's cup at the counter—successfully this time, with no spills. "There you go, sir. Enjoy."

Within the span of a minute, the door chimed twice more. *No end in sight,* Aimee thought, hurrying to pass sugar packets down the crowded counter. "I'm gonna need backup here," she called toward the kitchen. "Mary?"

Mary sidled out, uniform slightly wrinkled, a look on her face that hinted she'd rather be anywhere else. "I got it, I got it," she droned. "Don't expect miracles, Aims."

Aimee shot her a grateful look anyway. "No miracles needed —just help." She rattled off another order to the cook, then handled two quick payments at the register. Her feet already throbbed, yet she felt an undercurrent of satisfaction. *This* was her element: the rhythmic hustle of a busy diner, the hum of conversation, the swirl of stories passing through every day.

Mr. James cleared his throat pointedly. Aimee's head swiveled back to him and Mrs. Frank, who were bent together conspiratorially. "Something wrong, sir?" she asked, leaning over the counter.

They exchanged a meaningful look. Mrs. Frank nodded at Mr. James to speak. "You've been here a while," he began, dabbing pancake crumbs from his beard. "So they must keep you in the loop about the big stuff."

Aimee tensed, suspecting exactly where this was headed. "I might be in the loop," she ventured carefully, "depending on the topic."

Mr. James sighed. "It's Rochelle retiring—rumor says it's

happening soon." Mrs. Frank fiddled with her coffee cup, clearly worried. "If so, who's taking over?"

Aimee's heart gave a subtle lurch. She'd heard the whisperings, of course, but hearing them spoken aloud like this made it real. *This diner without Rochelle?* She tried to tamp down her unease. "No one's told me anything official," she replied, wiping the counter with brisk efficiency. "Honestly, my schedule hasn't changed. I'm still doing my usual shift. There's no sign of things turning upside down."

Mr. James leveled a curious gaze at her. Finally, he relaxed, shrugging. "Eh, maybe it's just gossip. Folks claim it might be Mary." He hitched a thumb at the kitchen door where Mary had disappeared.

Aimee snorted before she could stop herself. "Mary? Seriously?" She cringed inwardly when the swing door whooshed open, revealing Mary looking puzzled. "Did you call me?"

"No, sorry," Aimee replied quickly, clearing her throat.

Mary shrugged and slipped away again, announcing she was taking a break. The moment she was gone, Mr. James and Mrs. Frank burst into quiet chuckles, while Aimee rolled her eyes. "Teasing me won't make me spill secrets," she said good-humoredly. "Even if Rochelle does retire, it won't be overnight, and I doubt Mary would be first in line."

Mrs. Frank downed the last of her coffee with a thoughtful sigh. "Still, hard to imagine this place without Rochelle," she murmured. "She's the one who keeps the standards high, you know?"

Aimee nodded, a gentle sadness flickering in her chest. "Trust me, I know. She taught me everything about hospitality." For a moment, she stared out the wide window. Beyond the glass, autumn leaves spiraled gracefully to the pavement—little reminders that life changed whether you were ready or not. *Still,* she mused, *this diner is my comfort zone. Maybe someday I'll...*

She accidentally spoke a fragment of her thought aloud: "I could start my own catering company."

"Hmm? What's that, dear?" Mrs. Frank asked, brow quirking.

Flustered, Aimee shook off the reverie. "Oh—nothing, just daydreaming." She checked her watch, noticing lunch hour edged closer. "Aren't you running late yourself, Mrs. Frank?"

With a gasp, Mrs. Frank sprang from her stool. "Mercy, yes! The call center's waiting." She hustled out in a flurry of jacket sleeves, leaving a swirl of half-finished coffee behind.

Aimee waved goodbye, smiling after the older woman. The diner settled into a gentler midday lull—time enough for Aimee to breathe. The clock on the wall read noon, that sweet spot when the early crowds faded, leaving just a few scattered patrons sipping coffee or finishing meals.

She approached a pair of teen girls who were giggling over a shared dessert. "More chocolate cream pie? Or is that all for you two?" she asked kindly.

They beamed up at her, utensils tapping the empty plate. "That'll be all, thank you, Ms. Aimee."

Nodding, she prepared their check, setting the slips near the register. *Just one more hour,* she told herself. *Then I can go home, test out that new soup recipe, and wind down.*

She carried two slices of chocolate cream pie to the girls' table, politely excusing herself to fill a fresh coffee pot. *Steady as we go,* she reminded herself, relishing the calmer pace.

That was when the bell over the door chimed again.

Aimee turned, expecting a straggling regular. Instead, her feet rooted to the floor. The man who walked in was tall, with a comfortably confident stride that set him apart from most new faces who wandered in. He wore a simple beige sweater and well-fitted jeans, the casual combination somehow exuding easy sophistication. Everything about him, from his subtly over-grown hair to the crisp, bright aura around him, radiated an intriguing mix of city polish and laid-back warmth.

Time seemed to lag for a breath or two. Aimee's heart gave one unsteady jolt. *Who...?* She discreetly swallowed, her mind spinning through the diner's usual clientele. Definitely not someone she'd seen before. And she'd have remembered if she had—those brown eyes were enough to claim her full attention in a single glance.

He strolled to a booth near the windows. As soon as he settled, he scanned the menu with mild interest, occasionally looking around at the décor. Aimee took a steadying breath, but an involuntary warmth fluttered in her stomach. *Stop staring,* she scolded herself. *Mary can handle him.* She quickly spotted Mary juggling trays for the construction workers. *So much for that plan...*

Resigned, Aimee made her way over, determined to be friendly and composed. But the moment he looked up, she nearly forgot her practiced diner greeting. His face broke into the kind of effortless smile that made it feel like the two of them were the only ones in the room. A flutter of nerves raced through her—an unfamiliar sensation she couldn't quite quell.

"Hi," she managed, clearing her throat. "Welcome to Rochelle's Diner. Are you ready to order, or would you like a minute with the menu?"

He slid the laminated menu aside and focused on her with an unreadable but pleasant expression. "I think I'm good," he said in a low, warm hum. "Though it all looks tempting. Any chance you have a recommendation?"

Aimee found herself clutching her notepad as if it were a lifeline. "We have a chicken cheese sandwich that's pretty popular," she offered. *Don't overthink it,* she told herself, though her heart thumped with an odd urgency. "It's hearty, with just the right amount of sauce. Hard to go wrong."

His soft laugh sent a subtle buzz through her. "All right," he agreed. "If you say it's good, that's enough for me."

She nodded, forcing a gentle smile. "Great choice." Then, remembering to breathe, she asked, "Anything to drink?"

"Cherry soda, if you have it."

An unusual choice, but it suited the hint of playful spontaneity she sensed in him. "We do," she said. "I'll get that right out."

Spinning around, she returned to the kitchen, ignoring the knots that had formed between her ribs. *He's just a customer.* Still, she couldn't shake the heightened awareness trailing her thoughts. As she placed the order and found a bottle of cherry soda in the fridge, she silently counted her breaths: one, two, three.

Minutes later, she balanced a plate of fries and the sandwich on her arm, guiding a frosty soda glass with her other hand. The enticing aroma of melty cheese and warm bread accompanied her to his booth. "Here you go," she said, setting everything down.

He immediately picked up the sandwich, examining it with clear curiosity. Then he took a bite—and the soft, approving sound that escaped him made her shoulders ease. "Wow," he murmured, nodding. "That's really good. You were right."

Relief mingled with an unexpected spark of excitement. "Glad you like it. Let me know if you need anything else." She hovered a moment longer than necessary, oddly reluctant to walk away. But she shook herself free and took a step back. *Professional,* she reminded herself, giving him a brisk smile before she turned away.

In the quieter corner of the diner, she wiped down counters that didn't really need wiping, all the while sneaking glances to see how the newcomer fared. He ate at a leisurely pace, occasionally looking around as if soaking in the atmosphere. He didn't appear rushed or anxious—just entirely at ease. And each time she caught a glimpse of his profile, a fresh wave of curiosity tugged at her.

Why do I care so much? she asked herself. She'd vowed to keep things simple—no more heartbreak, no more chasing illusions. Yet the tiny hum of possibility flickered through her all the same.

Before her shift ended, she decided it was safer to let Mary handle the rest. "Hey," she muttered, catching Mary's elbow. "Table four's sandwich guy might need a drink refill. I'm about to clock out."

Mary's gaze flicked to him with mild intrigue. "Sure you don't want to say bye yourself?" she teased.

Aimee snorted—though the question stirred a pang of indecision inside her. "I'm positive," she said, forcing a casual shrug.

With that, she grabbed her purse and ducked through the back door into the alley. The crisp midday sun cast long shadows across the asphalt. Leaning against the brick wall, she closed her eyes, let out a breath, and tried to talk sense into her fluttering mind. *A random stranger with a charming smile.* That alone couldn't unravel the careful stability she'd built, right?

Her heart throbbed a faint protest, remembering the look in his brown eyes—like an invitation she hadn't dared answer. But no, it was too soon to slip into daydreams. She refused to risk her peace on a fleeting encounter. She had a life she loved and ambitions that didn't include heartbreak.

Stepping onto the sidewalk, she squared her shoulders and moved on, the memory of that low, inviting voice echoing in her thoughts. *He sure does look like the kind of window Nana used to talk about.*

But hope could be a tricky thing. She shook her head, marching toward her old minivan. *Stay practical, Aimee.* The autumn air felt cooler against her warm cheeks, as if the breeze itself tried to soothe her swirling emotions. If he ever came back, then maybe... but for now, she had recipes to test and a safe life to cherish.

In the hush of early afternoon, she opened the van door,

settled behind the wheel, and let the last few minutes replay in her mind. A single encounter, and somehow she felt a spark of possibility flickering in her chest. Her lips curved into a wry, small smile.

Don't get ahead of yourself, she whispered. With one more calming breath, she turned the key. The engine rumbled to life, and she pulled away from the diner, hoping to bury any silly, hopeful thoughts back in the bustle of her daily routine.

Yet no matter how she tried, the memory of that easy, confident stranger clung to her mind—like a sweet swirl of cherry soda she couldn't quite forget.

CHAPTER FOUR

*B*ack at his apartment, Malakai leaned back in his chair, letting the soft creak of the wood punctuate the quiet. He was still turning over his visit to Rochelle's Diner in his mind—especially the sandwich that had surprised him with its layered flavors and comforting familiarity. *Anyone* could slap together bread, cheese, and shredded chicken, but there'd been an unmistakable spark in that dish, like it had been prepared by someone who cared about every bite.

He suspected that "someone" might be Aimee.

Drumming his silver pen against the edge of a yellow notepad, Malakai cast a glance at the bold, blue-ink words he'd scrawled: **Seasonal specials**. A neat half-dozen ideas sloped beneath that heading—concepts to refresh the diner's menu, pulling in new crowds without losing the locals. Even as he examined them, he found his mind drifting elsewhere.

Her name was Aimee.

He let the word echo in his thoughts, recalling the moment he first spotted her. The morning bustle in the diner had felt vibrant—customers chatting, utensils clinking, the air fragrant with fresh coffee and sizzling bacon. Yet somehow, she'd stood out as if framed by a spotlight, her curls gently bouncing whenever she pivoted from the counter to the tables. She carried herself with a poised efficiency that spoke of years of diner work, but also radiated a subtle warmth he hadn't expected.

He remembered the brief brush of her presence—how her gentle perfume mingled with the aroma of bread and melted cheese when she set his plate in front of him. It had been a quiet, almost intimate moment in the midst of all that noise, and he couldn't shake it from his mind. And then there were her eyes—kind, yes, but behind the kindness lingered a hint of wistfulness he hadn't been able to ignore.

She's just a waitress, he told himself for what felt like the tenth time that evening. *A waitress who might unknowingly work for me.* But even that practical reminder didn't smother the curiosity sparking inside him. His pen kept tapping the notepad, creating a soft, rhythmic beat against the hush of the room.

A phone call broke through his thoughts. Malakai sighed, pressing the green icon. "Hey, Aunt Rochelle. What's going on?"

He pictured her bustling about the diner's office, probably packing up receipts or double-checking the schedule. Over the line, her voice carried its usual warmth. "Just wanted to see how your day went, baby. How'd your first little 'undercover' mission go?"

Malakai pushed aside the notepad and stood, crossing to the kitchen. "You really want to talk about my secret operation out loud?" he teased, opening the fridge. He grabbed a can of soda, the sharp hiss echoing through the speaker. "Hope no one's eavesdropping."

She gave a good-natured laugh. "Hush. I'm alone. So spill the beans. Did you get a decent picture of how everything's run?"

He popped the tab on the soda, then took a short sip. "I think so. The diner's in great shape—service is fast, customers look happy. Nothing glaring. But the menu might need a little push." He paused, thinking of that amazing sandwich. "It tastes wonderful, but we're missing variety. A little flair. Seasonal specials could do the trick."

Aunt Rochelle hmmed, followed by the telltale clank of metal on metal—maybe she was washing dishes or tidying up. "Hmm. Well, I know you've got ideas, Mr. City Consultant," she teased. "But you can't forget we feed the same local folks every day. Rattle them too much and they might think we're getting fancy on them."

Malakai closed the fridge, leaning his shoulder against it. "Don't worry—I'll tread carefully. Keep the classics, just add new twists." He inhaled, letting his mind flutter back to *her*. "Anyway, Mary didn't botch my order, if that's what you're worried about."

"She better not," Rochelle huffed. "That girl's on thin ice. I was half-expecting her to mess up. So if she didn't ruin your meal, what's lacking on the menu?"

Malakai smiled, imagining Aunt Rochelle's stern frown. "Like I said, it's not lacking flavor—just… novelty. We can't rely on the same old lineup forever. People love limited-time items, Aunt Rochelle. I think it'll bring extra business."

She went silent for a moment, then sighed. "All right, all right. I'll mull it over. Maybe do a little peach cobbler shake next summer, or a spiced pumpkin soup in the fall, that sort of thing. And hey—if a certain waitress has a good idea, you let me know. She might earn a raise if business picks up."

A gentle warmth unfurled in Malakai's chest at the mention of Aimee. She was more than just a friendly face. She'd been the one to recommend that chicken sandwich, apparently had a knack for cooking, too, and her quick, capable manner told him she played a bigger role than she let on. "She was definitely helpful," he admitted, trying not to sound too enthusiastic. "Welcoming and easy to talk to."

Rochelle's voice softened with approval. "That's Aimee in a nutshell. One of my best. She'll do anything for this place."

Malakai could almost see his aunt's satisfied nod through the phone. He tapped the top of the soda can, forcing himself to keep his tone casual. "Yeah, she struck me as someone who pours her heart into the job." He swallowed. "Anyway, I'll keep brainstorming the specials and pass my thoughts along soon."

"Sounds good, baby," Rochelle said. "I'm finishing up here. Are you dropping by tomorrow? Or do I gotta keep my distance to maintain your cover?"

He glanced at the clock—nearing nine p.m. He'd lost track of time in his musings. "I'll come by for lunch," he said. "If you see me, don't wave me over. I'll find a seat and watch from the sidelines, okay?"

She chuckled. "Understood, Mr. Spy. Sleep well, Malakai. Love you."

"Love you, too," he replied softly. Then, pressing the end button, he was left alone with his thoughts—and that persistent memory of Aimee's soft gaze.

Setting his phone aside, he let out a long breath. The silence of his apartment felt especially thick now. He rose and stepped into the bathroom, flipping on the light. As he brushed his teeth, his reflection stared back with an unreadable expression, his mind swirling with half-formed ideas about business strategy… and a growing curiosity about one particular waitress.

He pictured Aimee's face from earlier: the sudden lift of her brows when she noticed him, the way her voice had a slight catch at first, like she'd been momentarily taken aback. And that *spark* in her eyes—a blend of caution and kindness, as though she was used to being friendly but also knew how to guard her heart. It intrigued him more than it should have. Especially since *he* was the one who'd decided to keep his identity and intentions hidden.

I can't let myself get distracted, he reminded himself firmly, turning on the faucet to rinse. Splashes of cool water washed away the toothpaste, but not the flicker of interest that clung to his thoughts. It wasn't fair to her—or to the diner—to let personal fascination derail his purpose.

He toweled off, then wandered to the bedroom. The overhead light cast a soft glow on the stack of boxes he still needed to unpack. Posters from old conferences, a couple of trophies from his university days—he'd been planning to arrange them somewhere, but they remained untouched. It occurred to him that maybe he was ready for *new* mementos now, new pieces of life that weren't all about his past achievements.

Sliding under the covers, Malakai couldn't resist one last backward glance at the notepad resting on the table. A small swirl doodled next to Aimee's name, a testament to the way his mind had drifted while thinking of her. He told himself the interest was purely professional—she had potential, a creative streak, and knowledge that might help the diner stand out.

But as he settled into the pillow, his heart acknowledged there was more beneath the surface: a gentle pull that made him wonder about the woman behind that bright uniform and easy smile. She clearly had layers he wanted to uncover. The fleeting shadow in her eyes suggested she carried her own secrets, too.

"Focus, Malakai," he whispered to the dimly lit room. Rochelle's Diner needed him—his aunt was on the cusp of retirement, and the business had to be strong enough to thrive without her. That was his top priority. No matter how much a certain waitress and her quiet, wistful expression lingered in his thoughts.

Tomorrow would bring another chance to observe the diner's ebb and flow, test more menu items, and refine his plans. *And maybe,* a small voice in his head added, *it'll bring another glimpse of Aimee.*

With that, Malakai breathed deeply, forcing his mind to settle on the ticking clock and the gentle hum of traffic outside. He closed his eyes, determined to drift off before his thoughts circled back to that smile again. *He had a job to do, after all,* he reminded himself, as the darkness of sleep crept in.

But still, in the quiet spaces between wake and dream, her image floated in his memory—a bright face, warm laugh, and the sweet fragrance of optimism and longing, all rolled into one. And despite himself, Malakai found he couldn't be entirely sorry that she'd stolen a corner of his focus. Not tonight, anyway.

CHAPTER FIVE

*A*imee glanced at her watch, confirming she still had another hour and a half left in her shift. *Just a little longer*, she coached herself. Rolling the tension from her neck, she mustered a bright smile that she hoped hid any trace of fatigue.

All around her, the midday crowd ebbed and flowed. A group of office workers congregated at the counter, loudly sharing weekend gossip over half-empty mugs of coffee. Two booths down, a mom tried to keep her energetic toddler from tossing crayons onto the sticky floor. Through it all, the savory scent of frying bacon mingled with the sweetness of syrup and sugar—traces of Rochelle's diner magic lingering in every corner.

A voice called her name. "Aimee! Over here!" rang out in a cheery lilt.

She spun toward one of the round-topped tables and spotted Nevaeh Carr, a friendly face from her high school days. *Unexpected*, but welcome. "Hey, Nevaeh," Aimee greeted, pocketing her notepad in a rush of curiosity. "Been a while since we last caught up."

Nevaeh's giggle sparkled in the midday sunlight that filtered through the broad windows. "Too long, honestly. But I couldn't let you clock out before ordering my favorite salad. You're the only one who does it justice."

Despite the bustle, Aimee felt a gentle glow spread through her chest. The memory of Nevaeh's high school hijinks—her charm, her clumsiness, and her irrepressible spirit—drifted back. "Oh, the roasted white bean salad? It's been a minute since I've made that." She pursed her lips, though delight tugged at the corners of her mouth. "But for you, no problem."

"Thank you," Nevaeh said, relief and excitement shining in her eyes. "I've been craving it for weeks."

Aimee scribbled the order in her pad. "Anything to drink?"

Nevaeh tapped her chin dramatically. "Orange juice this time—gotta be a little healthier after having Khalil. My body's on a new schedule these days."

"I bet," Aimee replied with a grin. "You look great, by the way. Motherhood suits you." She gave a small, admiring nod to Nevaeh's flawlessly draped blouse. "I'm impressed you still have time to dress up."

The woman's laugh was warm, carrying just a hint of self-consciousness. "Trust me, it took a while. I'm definitely softer around the middle, but I'll take all the cuddles with my baby boy. It's worth every extra inch."

Aimee chuckled, then clutched her notepad close. "Let me work my salad magic. Be right back."

In the kitchen, she slid into her "fill-in cook" rhythm. Chopped red onions and crisp greens joined lightly seasoned white beans in a stainless-steel bowl. She whisked up a tangy dressing—her secret was a dash of honey and a bit more garlic than standard recipes called for. The medley of scents rose, hitting her nose with a rich, zesty warmth that always made her mouth water.

When she returned to the dining area, her cheeks glowed

from the heat of the stoves, but pride lifted her steps. "Here we are," she announced, setting the bowl in front of Nevaeh. "One nutritious salad, made with extra care."

Nevaeh's face lit up as though Aimee had just delivered a five-star meal. "It looks perfect," she said, wiggling her fork in excitement. "Thank you!"

About to reply, Aimee felt her gaze drift across the diner—and froze when it landed on the tall stranger she'd served days before. He was back, seated by the windows, his profile in partial shadow. *That same posture... that same polished ease.* Her heart clenched unexpectedly.

Why's he here again so soon? A small thrill ran through her veins, the memory of their brief chats flaring bright in her mind. She forced herself to focus on Nevaeh—who had begun wolfing down the salad with an enthusiasm that was equal parts amusing and flattering.

"I think I taste even more garlic this time," Nevaeh enthused. "It's awesome!"

Aimee grinned, handing her a napkin. "Wipe that dressing off your lip, girl," she teased. "I can't have you scaring the other customers away with a sauce mustache." Yet behind her playful tone, her thoughts kept tugging back to the newcomer in the booth.

Her curiosity, as well as a hint of nerves, coiled in the pit of her stomach. *All right, we can't just stand here gawking.* "Enjoy," Aimee said. "And say hi to Tia, Sean, and Khalil for me."

Leaving Nevaeh to her meal, she forced her feet to carry her toward the booth. A current of heat rippled through her chest. Even from a few steps away, she noticed again the subtle lines of his face, the gentle slant of his brows, and that impeccably trimmed facial hair. The midday sun, pouring through the window, traced along his cheekbones in a way that made Aimee's heart flutter.

"Welcome back," she managed, relieved her voice stayed level. "Nice to see you again."

He looked up, a flicker of recognition in his warm hazel eyes. "I decided to stop by for lunch," he said, tone as easy as the faintest breeze. "Can't stay away from good food, I guess."

"Well, the more the merrier," Aimee replied, slipping her pen from its place behind her ear. "If you become a regular, you might even earn some special privileges."

His gaze followed the motion of her hand, perhaps noticing how she fiddled with her pen when she was nervous. "Special privileges?" he echoed, a light note of teasing in his voice.

She nodded toward where Nevaeh sat, still inhaling the salad. "We sometimes do custom orders for folks we know well —like a points program," she joked. Her heart thumped a little louder, noticing the way his eyes glimmered at the explanation.

"Ah, I see," he said, a smile tugging at his lips. "Well, maybe I'll have to work my way up to that." He laid the menu down. "In the meantime, any suggestions? You didn't steer me wrong last time."

He liked my pick, she thought with a small swell of pride. She remembered how he'd practically devoured the sandwich, each bite met with clear approval. Maybe it shouldn't matter so much, but it did. "How about a chicken pesto panini?" she offered. "We grill it with roasted peppers and drizzle it with our house sauce. Crisp on the outside, gooey in the middle, plus a hint of smoke to keep it interesting."

"Sounds perfect," he answered, setting aside the menu. "I look forward to seeing if it measures up."

Her skin tingled under the warmth of his stare. *Get it together, Aimee.* "Sure thing," she managed. "I'll tell the kitchen, and we'll see if we can impress you again."

She pivoted toward the cooking station, heart thrumming an uneven beat. Brushing past Mary, who was halfheartedly wiping counters, Aimee felt her coworker's watchful gaze.

"Who is that?" Mary asked under her breath. "He's got you tripping over your words, Aims. You never stutter."

"Me?" Aimee forced a short laugh. "You're imagining things."

Mary's brow lifted with skepticism. "I see how you keep glancing at him."

Aimee pressed her lips together, refusing to feed Mary's curiosity. She snatched a glass for orange juice, ignoring the faint flush creeping up her neck. *It's nothing.* She refused to dissect the flush of heat the stranger caused whenever he set that warm, intent gaze on her.

Just as Aimee finished filling another customer's drink, the cook hollered, "Pesto panini, table seven!"

Her pulse spiked again. *Here we go.* Grabbing the plate, she wove around the booths toward him. The diner's ambient noise momentarily faded, replaced by the rush of her own heartbeat.

"Here you go," she said, placing the plate before him with all the composure she could muster. The sandwich's roasted peppers contrasted strikingly against the golden bread. "Enjoy."

His eyes flicked between the dish and her face. "Smells fantastic," he said. "Thank you, Aimee." The way he spoke her name felt deliberate—almost intimate.

She felt the heat bloom across her cheeks. Part of her wanted to ask if he'd read her nametag. But the sincerity in his tone told her otherwise. "We pride ourselves on speed and flavor," she offered lightly, stepping back. Then, summoning a small burst of bravery: "If you end up liking it, you might really need to become a regular."

His smile deepened, almost playful. "I'm considering it more and more."

Before she could dwell on that, a beckoning wave from another table forced her away. The hours she spent here had taught her how to juggle multiple tasks—refilling drinks, clearing plates, and taking orders all at once. Yet all afternoon, her focus wavered, drifting back to *him* every few minutes.

Whenever she stole a glance, he was either savoring the panini or watching her with quiet interest. Every time their gazes brushed, a thrill skipped through her nerves, leaving her breathless.

It was ridiculous, really, how much it affected her. But as she distributed fresh napkins to a frazzled mother whose child had spilled a cup of juice, she caught herself silently hoping he'd linger—stay just a little longer, so she could glimpse that contented expression again.

Within a quarter hour, the last crumbs of his meal disappeared. She let herself look one final time before heading to the counter. Her thoughts tangled with questions she couldn't fully form: *Is he passing through? Does he live nearby now? Why does it feel so... easy when he's around?*

She tried to banish the internal chatter. A random stranger's presence shouldn't send her heart into a spin—she knew better, especially after the heartbreaks she'd endured. Yet the buoyant warmth in her chest was hard to ignore. Perhaps, *just maybe*, letting her guard slip a little wouldn't be so bad.

That flutter of hope made her lips curve into a reluctant smile as she wiped down a table. She'd see where things went—if anywhere at all. For now, the gentle promise in his voice, the casual way he said her name, the quiet thrill that sparked whenever she felt his gaze… it all made the long shift feel decidedly sweeter.

And as she passed the booth one last time, her breath caught at the subtle nod he gave her. *Yes*, she thought, *maybe he will come back... and that might be exactly what I need right now.*

CHAPTER SIX

Malakai still couldn't shake the memory of that panini, even as he sat back and folded his utensils neatly on the now-empty plate. The soft crunch of the grilled bread, the tangy spread that cradled each bite, the warmth it left in his chest—it felt almost surreal to be this enamored with a sandwich. But he was.

He propped an elbow on the table, releasing a hushed "wow" that blended with the low hum of the diner. Whatever alchemy went into that dish had lulled him into an unexpected midday stupor. *Borderline magical.* He normally never considered a post-lunch nap, but that panini had been both satisfying and comforting, like a gentle hug for his soul.

With a sweep of his gaze, Malakai observed the steady traffic of customers. Servers in pastel uniforms bustled with trays of soda and plates of fries, while patrons chatted animatedly or quietly savored their meals. A faint clatter of silverware on ceramic added a familiar soundtrack of productivity. From the corner of his eye, he noticed Aimee tending the counter, effortlessly pouring juice for a regular who joked with her like an old friend. The easy grace in her posture—no pretense, no forced hospitality—drew his attention more than he intended.

Just then, as though sensing his thoughts, Aimee glanced over. Their eyes locked. In that flicker of shared surprise, Malakai felt his breath catch. Time seemed to slow for an instant, a pleasant pressure building in his chest. *She's even more striking when she's not in motion,* he thought, noticing the bright curiosity that lit up her features.

Her eyes rounded slightly, as if she hadn't expected him to be watching. She hesitated, then crossed the diner toward him, notepad in hand. Her polite, focused expression carried the slightest edge of nerves—enough to make him want to ease her concerns.

"Everything all right, sir?" she asked, a subtle quiver in her voice. "Looks like you're done."

He nudged the empty plate forward. "Yes, I'm definitely finished." A grin curved his lips. "It tasted like something angels might serve in heaven."

A flash of amusement softened her posture. "I think you might be spoiling us with that kind of praise," she teased. "But I'm really glad you enjoyed it. We try to treat everyone like kings and queens here—though angels, that's a new one."

Malakai chuckled, relishing how easily her sense of humor surfaced. "It's well-deserved," he said simply. "I can tell you care about this place. You seem…happy here."

An appreciative glow brightened her eyes. "I do love it. If I didn't, I'd go stir-crazy showing up every day. There are plenty of other jobs in Sweetgum, but this diner's like my second home." She gave a small shrug, as though trying to downplay the devotion in her voice.

He watched the soft bounce of her curls and the delicate set of her features. She carried a certain spark he couldn't quite name. "I'll bet a woman like you has lots of options," he found himself saying. The words came out more candidly than he intended. Quickly, he added, "So what makes you stay? Is it just the food, or something else?"

She paused, gathering her thoughts. A faint wistfulness crossed her expression before she answered, "Food is…everything to me. I love how it can transform a day, mend a mood, bring people together." Her gaze flicked to the plate, then back up to Malakai's face. "I don't want to be stuck in the kitchen all the time, even though I adore cooking. I like being part of the entire experience. Handing someone a plate, seeing that first reaction—it's priceless."

He nodded slowly, feeling an unexpected connection to her enthusiasm. "It's incredible how something so simple—like a good meal—can set the tone for everything else in life," he said. The gentle rumble of conversation in the background made their exchange feel strangely intimate, as though the rest of the diner receded.

Aimee exhaled a shy laugh. "Exactly," she agreed softly. Then her cheeks flushed with self-consciousness. "I ramble sometimes when I get passionate about this stuff. Sorry."

"Don't be," Malakai replied, warmth filling his tone. "I like hearing it."

She studied him for a quiet beat, then cleared her throat. "So, since we're basically swapping food philosophies, maybe we should do an actual introduction?" She set her notepad aside and offered her hand. "I'm Aimee."

He gently took her hand in his, instantly aware of its softness. "Malakai," he said, using only his first name, an echo of caution tugging at his mind. But there was a pang—maybe longing—wishing he could say more. Letting her in on his full reason for being here felt impossibly tempting, yet he couldn't sabotage his plan or Rochelle's trust.

They lingered for a beat, his hand enveloping hers. A quiet thrill stirred in his chest, the warmth of her skin tugging at his own composure. Reluctantly, he released her fingers. "Nice to meet you properly."

Aimee tucked a curl behind her ear, as if unsettled by the moment, too. "You as well," she said lightly. "Though I figured out your name from that old register slip earlier—Malakai's not exactly common. But it's nice to hear you say it."

He couldn't hide a small smile. *She'd noticed more than he realized.* "So," he said, clearing his throat. "I'm guessing you enjoy cooking as much as serving, right?"

A gentle pride sparked in her eyes. "Definitely. Actually…I made the sauce you tasted today. It's my own recipe."

Malakai straightened, intrigued. "Wait, seriously? That sauce was all you?" He tapped the table for emphasis. "I mean it when I say you could market that. It's incredible."

A hint of rose colored her cheeks at the compliment. "Thanks," she murmured. "I'm always tinkering with flavors. Glad to know it's hitting the mark."

He leaned in a fraction, lowering his voice. "It's more than hitting the mark—it's a home run," he said in earnest. "Why aren't you in the back cooking? Seems like that's where you'd really shine."

She cast a glance at the line of hungry patrons. "I get that question a lot," she admitted. "But I need both sides of it— kitchen creativity and connecting with people. It's sweeter that way. Kind of like having my cake and eating it, too." Her face brightened with playful sincerity. "And chatting with you is part of the fun," she added lightly, her gaze flitting down almost shyly.

Malakai's pulse gave a slight hiccup. An irrational wave of jealousy surfaced at the idea that she might talk to *everyone* like this—but he tamped it down. No sense in being possessive of a woman he'd just met. "So do you chat with everyone?" he asked with a half smile, pretending a casual tone.

She laughed, a genuine, bright sound that made the diner's

hum seem quieter. "Pretty much," she admitted. "Welcome to Sweetgum: no secrets, especially within these walls."

He glanced around at the smiling, familiar faces. "I see," he murmured. "Well, I have a different question for you. Have you ever suggested new dishes for the official menu? Something beyond your sauce, maybe a unique weekly special?"

A flicker of excitement and surprise crossed her features. "Funny you should mention that. A few customers have nudged me to bring new ideas to the manager. I guess I'm just never sure if it's my place—Rochelle runs a tight ship, and the menu's worked for ages."

Malakai drummed a thoughtful beat on the table, careful to keep his "undercover" objective hidden. "A menu that's already good can still be better," he said softly. "And if anyone's got the skill to elevate it, it's you."

Her eyes sparkled at his unwavering confidence. "Maybe I'll finally pitch a few recipes," she said, modestly fiddling with the notepad. "Thanks for the nudge."

He offered a small, encouraging nod. "Anytime." His gaze slid to the empty plate. "Clearly, I'm on your side when it comes to taste-testing."

Aimee chuckled, lifting his plate and glass with practiced ease. "We'll see how bold I get, I guess." She stepped back, giving him a tiny wave. "Enjoy the rest of your day, Malakai. Thanks for coming in."

He watched her weave around tables, heading for the kitchen drop-off. A swirl of possibilities danced in his head— ideas for new seasonal dishes, promotional events, ways to highlight Aimee's talent. But amid the practical business angles, a gentle current of fascination tugged him deeper.

There was something undeniably special about her—an openheartedness layered with quiet determination. It made him want to learn more about her story, to see what else might make her eyes glow with that fervent spark.

As the afternoon light shifted across the diner, Malakai felt a renewed optimism seep into his bones. The plan to revitalize Rochelle's Diner was taking shape in his mind, but now it wasn't just about business. Aimee's passion for food—and her presence—made everything feel more alive.

Leaning back in the booth, he gathered his thoughts. Undercover or not, this was the first time in a while he felt excited about a project beyond the spreadsheets and strategy. If Aimee was the key to transforming the menu, then maybe she was also the key to making *him* see Sweetgum with new eyes.

He rose and left a generous tip on the table before stepping into the gentle afternoon sun. As he headed to his car, one last thought lingered: he was already looking for an excuse to return. And *Aimee* was at the center of that pull—she had a spark he couldn't ignore.

His next steps in Sweetgum, it seemed, might revolve around more than just saving a diner's legacy. There was something else waiting in the wings—something bright, warm, and undeniably thrilling. And Malakai couldn't wait to see where it led.

CHAPTER SEVEN

"I'm so glad we managed to grab lunch together," Maia said, twirling her noodles around her chopsticks with practiced ease. The midday crowd provided a cozy hum in the background: servers weaving between tables, the light clink of bowls against tabletops, and a subtle sizzle emanating from the open kitchen. The air swelled with the aromas of soy, garlic, and something sweetly spiced—hallmarks of the Zhang family's culinary flair.

Aimee tilted her head as she watched the swirl of steam rising from her own bowl of spicy lā miàn. "When your shift changed," Maia continued, "I worried we'd have to skip our usual meet-ups, but it actually lines up perfectly with my lunch break. Even if it means you have to be up before the sun…"

Aimee let out a playful groan around a forkful of noodles. Despite her love of cooking, waking at four in the morning was never easy, but she'd do it for the job she adored. "Who said I have a problem with the early shift?" she teased, dabbing her mouth with a napkin. "I get to see Sweetgum at its quietest. There's a charm in that."

She glanced around the restaurant, taking in the harmonious

chatter. Families clustered at round tables, passing steaming dishes and sharing laughter, while a few couples leaned in close, lost in private conversation. A contented sigh escaped her. These were the moments she loved—moments where a simple meal transformed into quality time.

"Oh, I don't know…" Maia said, eyes sparkling. "You might've mentioned it once or twice when we were in college. The coffee-fueled ramblings, remember?"

Aimee snorted softly, recalling how she and Maia used to pull all-nighters while huddled in the dorm kitchen, each venting about their day and concocting spontaneous midnight snacks. "Maybe so," she conceded. "But back then, we stayed up too late studying—or watching those random reality shows you loved—so I had an excuse."

"Touché," Maia shot back with a grin. She wound more noodles around her chopsticks, pausing to inhale the fragrant steam. "Anyway, thanks for tagging along for the dress stuff later. Wedding planning is no joke. Alex is supportive, but there are so many little details, it makes my head spin. At least I know we'll have a good laugh afterward."

Aimee dipped her spoon into the spicy broth, savoring the zesty scent that danced up to her nose. Chili flakes and garlic teased her taste buds. "I'm thrilled to come. And I love hearing you gush about Alex stepping up. So many brides complain at the diner that their fiancés won't help at all—but you two really share the workload."

Maia's cheeks warmed with obvious happiness. "It's our wedding, not just mine," she said, rolling her chopsticks to gather another mouthful. "He might meet us at the boutique if he can wrap up his conference call early. I'm still a little nervous, though. Everyone raves about this place, but you never know if a dress will *feel* right until you try it on."

Aimee shrugged lightly, taking a careful bite of her noodles. A flash of heat tickled her throat, and she reached for her water glass. "If people hype it up," she reasoned, "there's probably a good reason. Besides, I'm sure you'll look stunning no matter what. You're basically glowing these days."

A flicker of gratitude shone in Maia's eyes as she set her chopsticks down. "Have I told you lately how much I appreciate you? Because I really do. But..." Her tone softened, as though steeling herself for a delicate question. "Promise me something—be honest: do you ever feel like a third wheel when Alex is around?"

Aimee blinked, momentarily caught off guard. "Third wheel?" She stirred her spoon in the broth, watching a swirl of chili oil rise to the surface. "Honestly? No. I'm happy to see you thriving. After how rough things got post-divorce... you deserve all the joy Alex brings."

She recalled those harder days: Maia's puffy eyes, tear-stained cheeks, and the trembling heartbreak that only a failed marriage could incite. But that was all in the past now. "Seeing you and Alex is a reminder that second chances happen," Aimee added, smiling. "It makes me want to give him a trophy for best fiancé ever."

The tenderness in Maia's gaze spoke volumes. "Thanks, Aims. You've been there through every bump. I'd never want you to feel overshadowed."

A gentle hush passed between them—a moment of shared understanding. The sizzle of woks in the background, the clatter of plates, the low hum of other patrons chatting all seemed to fade for a heartbeat. Aimee sensed the sincerity brimming behind Maia's words. *She really does worry about me,* Aimee thought affectionately.

"Well," Maia resumed, leaning in with a conspiratorial air, "we've talked enough about me—what about you? Anything exciting on the horizon? Any new prospects in the love department?"

Aimee set her fork down, letting out a small, wry chuckle. "Open doors and no windows," she muttered, half to herself.

"Come again?" Maia asked, eyes narrowing playfully.

Aimee steeled herself with a breath. "You know that saying, 'When one door closes, another opens'? I've been thinking lately about how your first marriage ended but then Alex came along, almost like a window of opportunity you didn't expect." She tucked a stray curl behind her ear, watching a couple near the front pay their bill and leave, hands linked. "But for me, maybe that door-and-window logic doesn't apply. I have a good job, friends, cooking—enough to fill my life. I'm not missing anything."

Maia reached across the table, warm hand covering Aimee's. "There's nothing wrong with counting your blessings," she said gently. "But you're allowed to hope for more, too."

"I'm fine, Mai. Really," Aimee insisted, though her voice wavered slightly. "Some heartbreaks just teach you to appreciate what you have. I've had enough dead ends to know love isn't guaranteed, no matter how badly you want it." She shrugged to hide the small knot tightening in her chest. "I promise, I'm not depressed about it. I'm just... realistic."

With a soft sigh, Maia squeezed her fingers once and withdrew. "As long as you're truly content. But I know you, Aimee. That heart of yours is bigger than you admit. Don't lock it away entirely."

To break the tension, Aimee raised her spoon in mock seriousness. "Yes, ma'am. I'll keep it cracked open just a hair." She managed a reassuring smile, then nudged their conversation back to wedding details—flower arrangements, bridesmaid dresses, color palettes. They finished their bowls in comfortable chatter, each reveling in the heat of the aromatic broth.

Eventually, they settled the bill at the cashier near the door. The hostess, a short woman with a beaming smile, thanked them profusely for visiting. The glass doors swung open onto

Sweetgum's bustling Main Street, where the crisp fall air carried the earthy scent of leaves. A teenage employee in an apron was sweeping the sidewalk, though the swirling gust of golden foliage made it a losing battle.

Aimee paused beneath the canopy of brilliant orange and gold leaves overhead. Autumn always felt bittersweet to her—warm colors, cooler winds, and the gentle reminder that life pressed forward, seasons changing whether you were ready or not. She inhaled deeply, letting the crisp air fill her lungs. *Focus on the present*, she told herself, trailing after Maia.

Within minutes, they reached a boutique with sleek glass windows. Warm light spilled out, revealing mannequins draped in satin gowns and the glimmer of rhinestone embellishments. A dainty bell chimed as they stepped inside, the plush carpet muffling their footsteps. A soft, floral perfume—likely lavender—drifted through the air, giving the space a gentle, almost spa-like atmosphere.

Alex stood near a polished glass counter, skimming a bridal magazine while chatting with the store clerk. Tall racks of wedding dresses formed a mini labyrinth, each garment encased in a protective plastic cover. Aimee couldn't help but smile at the mini chandelier hanging overhead, casting dappled sparkles across the walls.

"Well, look who's here," Alex greeted, setting the magazine aside. He slipped an arm around Maia's waist, pressing a quick kiss to her temple. "Glad you both could make it."

"Thanks for waiting," Aimee said, returning his friendly nod. "You look pretty relaxed for a guy who's about to make a thousand wedding decisions."

Alex chuckled. "The key is delegating," he joked, exchanging an affectionate glance with Maia. "Just ask Maia—she's the real captain here. I'm just the loyal first mate."

Maia shook her head in amusement. "Don't let him fool you. He's been a big help." Together, they stepped toward a display of shimmering gowns, each one spotlighted by a soft overhead beam. The store clerk, a perky young woman named Denise, arrived to discuss possible fits and fabrics. She ushered Maia into a fitting room to take measurements while Alex scrolled through a wedding app on his phone.

"Don't mind me," Aimee teased, sinking into a plush loveseat along the wall. "I'll just admire the décor and make encouraging noises."

Alex checked his watch, suddenly grimacing. "Actually, I need to jump on a conference call soon," he said. "I thought I'd have more time before the meeting. Maia, I'll be outside, okay?" He excused himself with a fond wave in Aimee's direction, phone pressed to his ear.

Aimee watched him depart, letting her gaze skim the boutique's interior. Velvet drapes shielded a set of mirrored podiums, presumably for brides to stand on while testing out the full effect of a gown. A hush of reverence seemed to fill the space—something about wedding dresses always felt steeped in promise and dreams.

After a few minutes, Maia emerged, her eyes shining with excitement. "Denise says they have a fabric similar to what I tried on at the last shop but in a style that might suit me better." She gestured toward a flowing gown on a mannequin, the skirt whisper-light and delicately pleated. "I never thought I'd like something so… ethereal. It feels unreal."

Aimee got to her feet, stepping closer to run her fingertips over the gauzy fabric. The texture was gentle, almost cloudlike. "Wow," she breathed, taking in the subtle shimmer that caught the overhead light. "It's stunning. I can already imagine you gliding down the aisle."

A faint flush rose in Maia's cheeks. "I'm nervous," she admitted quietly. "But in a good way, you know? Like, I've done this before, but with Alex, it's different. Everything just feels right."

Aimee reached out, giving her arm a comforting squeeze. "I'm happy for you, Mai. This time, it'll be perfect."

They wandered toward another rack displaying mermaid silhouettes and elaborate ball gowns. Maia mulled over different necklines while Aimee occasionally pointed out interesting details—lace backings, pearl-like buttons, embroidered bodices. A sleek trumpet-style gown made Maia's eyebrows lift in fascination. "Maybe," she murmured, half to herself.

The store's overhead music changed to a sweet instrumental track, and for a moment, Aimee let her mind drift. She envisioned how she'd feel trying on one of these gowns for herself. An old flicker of longing stirred—just a tiny spark she usually kept deeply hidden. *You're not made for that*, a voice in her head chided. *You don't do well with risking your heart.*

Her mouth tightened, and she focused back on Maia. "So, the tailor said this style might suit your figure," Aimee offered, gesturing to a nearby display of off-the-shoulder designs.

Maia took one off the rack, admiring it before hugging it to her chest. "I'll try it," she said, a glint of determination in her eyes. "Let's see if I can feel that 'wow' moment everyone talks about."

She was about to whisk off to the fitting room when she paused, fixing Aimee with a gentle look. "Hey," she murmured. "Just remember: love isn't a limited resource. There's plenty to go around, and you never know when it might wander in."

Aimee forced a quip to ease her own discomfort. "Wander in, like a lost tourist in Sweetgum? We don't get too many of those." Despite her teasing tone, a sudden image of the handsome diner newcomer crossed her mind, unbidden. She pressed her lips together, determined not to divulge anything further.

With a small smirk, Maia gave her a knowing grin. "Uh-huh, sure. Well, let me try this on. Wish me luck!" She disappeared behind the changing-room curtain.

Aimee, left on her own, ambled around the boutique. The

hush amplified the soft rustling of satin as a couple of other brides-to-be meandered through the racks. Occasionally, the whoosh of a curtain revealed glimpses of white fabric swirling around bodies.

The calm left her mind drifting back to him—that new customer who'd popped into Rochelle's Diner. Twice now, he'd greeted her with warm curiosity. And each time, she'd felt a small thrill stirring under her ribcage. *You never know when it might wander in,* Maia's voice echoed in her head.

"Or out," she muttered quietly, brushing her fingertips along a lace veil. Because for all she knew, he'd just as quickly vanish from Sweetgum and never return. He was, after all, just a newcomer, possibly here on temporary business. Letting her thoughts linger on him was risky. She'd built her life around the safety of routine. Heartaches of the past still loomed large in her memory.

Yet the faint swirl of excitement—like a gentle breeze tickling her senses—refused to be fully banished. She closed her eyes briefly, inhaling the faint lavender in the air, reminding herself she was happy for Maia and Alex, that was what mattered. Her own desires could stay locked away, for now.

By the time Maia reemerged, wearing a radiant smile and carrying a short list of possible dresses, Aimee found herself exhaling a mixture of relief and anticipation. The wedding talk, the plush gowns, the sweet smell of possibility—they all mingled into a single swirl of promise.

They stepped outside, meeting Alex on the sidewalk. He ended his call with a grin. "Find anything you love?" he asked Maia, tucking her hand into the crook of his arm.

"Potentially," Maia said, her voice trembling with excitement. "They're going to schedule a private fitting so I can choose between two styles."

Aimee nodded, smiling at the happy couple. *It's real,* she thought—Maia was well on her way to a future that fit her heart's desires. And that was enough to make Aimee's heart glow with contentment. Whatever else might be waiting—love, heartbreak, or mere contentment—she'd face it on her own terms. For now, supporting her friend was more than enough.

As they strolled down Main Street together, autumn leaves drifting in their wake, Aimee felt a small stirring of hope ignite despite herself. Because even if she claimed she wasn't searching for a "window," part of her couldn't help but crack it open just a smidge, curious about what fresh air might blow in.

CHAPTER EIGHT

"And send." Malakai's finger tapped the keyboard one last time, dispatching his final email of the morning. He shifted in his home office chair and lifted his coffee cup—dark roast, no sugar—to his lips. The rich, almost bitter warmth slid across his tongue, reigniting his senses after a flurry of administrative tasks. Outside his window, a blanket of gray clouds hinted at an impending drizzle, yet the muted sky only sharpened his focus on the mission at hand.

He set the mug down on the smooth surface of his small desk, scanning the icons on his laptop. Early though it was, the day felt laden with promise—and a hint of tension. Today was critical: his aunt, Rochelle, would be officially announcing her retirement at the diner around ten o'clock. His mind spun with questions about how the news would ripple through Sweetgum. He could practically envision the diner employees' reactions, the patrons' murmurs of speculation, and the swirl of half-formed rumors taking flight.

One week after that, Malakai would formally step in to fill Rochelle's shoes. Family member. Signed, sealed, delivered. He flexed his shoulders, trying to shrug off the tight anticipation that coiled in them. *The whole town's about to discover Rochelle has kin they never knew existed.* He couldn't guess how they'd respond, but that was part of the thrill. And a small measure of anxiety, too.

A ghost of a smile tugged at his lips. He might not be a classic Sweetgum local, but he understood just how beloved Rochelle's Diner was. Whether they welcomed him or not, he'd do his best to steer it into the future. *I don't need their approval,* he reminded himself. Yet an inexplicable prickle of need pressed in his chest. Maybe he didn't require unanimous love, but a modicum of respect—*that* would be nice.

With a tiny sigh, he glanced down at his t-shirt—a relic from his boarding school days, sporting a cracked emblem on the chest. Those years felt so distant now, but the memory of leaving home for that campus sometimes overlapped with how he felt returning to Sweetgum: a swirl of uncertainty and excitement all at once. Despite his professional success, he was still forging a personal identity, step by hesitant step.

He shook free of the introspection and reread the email he'd sent earlier to the diner's manager, Mr. Germaine. Technically, the manager believed he was following instructions from an anonymous benefactor—someone aiming to assist with new marketing and menu ideas in Rochelle's absence. Malakai almost laughed at how cloak-and-dagger it felt. *This undercover approach is overkill, isn't it?* But as soon as he questioned it, he reminded himself of the logic: he needed unvarnished insight into how the diner ran, how staff adapted to new policies, and how customers responded. Revealing his identity too soon might muddy the waters with deference and pretense.

He snorted under his breath. "What's wrong with me?" he mused, half-amused, half-exasperated by his own elaborate plan. Maybe getting older made him crave a bit more fun. This entire scheme—even down to the secret instructions for Mr.

Germaine—brought a certain spark to his otherwise calculated life.

His coffee, still warm, beckoned him for another sip. As he lifted the mug, the unexpected memory of Aimee's smile flashed behind his eyes. A small pang of surprise flicked through him. Had he really let his mind stray so easily? He traced the faint swirl pattern on the mug with his thumb, then set it down harder than intended. The cup rattled, sending a stray droplet of coffee onto the counter.

"Focus," he muttered, wiping the small spill. *Aimee* had been on his mind more than he cared to admit, her laughter and her unassuming confidence playing across his thoughts. He tried to frame it in professional terms—she was a key resource for potential new dishes, an integral part of the diner's future. But he couldn't deny there was something else. Something that kept his attention snagged on the memory of her curls, her quick wit, and that subtle aura of longing in her eyes.

His phone screen lit up with a reminder, snapping him back to the present. *Dinner at Rochelle's—7:00 p.m.* Perfect. Time to get some real work done before then. He rolled his shoulders again, determined to use every bit of daylight for his planning. But no matter how many times he opened spreadsheets or typed out new ideas, his mind drifted to what might be happening at the diner that very moment. *The announcement,* he reminded himself. Maybe it was already out, sending waves through Sweetgum. And Aimee... how would she react?

He forced himself to minimize the mental tangent, hunkering down to solidify the new marketing proposals. If all went well, he'd have them fully prepped by the time he formally stepped in, ensuring an immediate rollout that could boost the diner's reputation beyond local circles. The hours passed in a blur of typing, phone calls, and scheduling—punctuated by the occasional daydream of the diner's warm atmosphere and the swirl of coffee-scented air.

~

MALAKAI ARRIVED at Aunt Rochelle's place just as dusk began painting the sky with muted purple and orange streaks. The front porch light glowed, guiding him into the familiar warmth of her home. He could almost taste the nostalgia in the air: the faint hint of lemon cleaner, the cozy clutter of old trinkets, and the comforting resonance of a house that had remained mostly unchanged for decades.

"Malakai, baby!" Rochelle called from the kitchen the moment she heard him close the door. He followed the savory scent of roasting chicken, mouth watering in anticipation. Entering the cramped yet welcoming dining area, he spotted her at the stove, apron tied snug around her waist, dishing out a platter of steaming goodness.

He greeted her with a quick hug, inhaling the comforting blend of spices and thyme that clung to her apron. "Smells incredible. You sure know how to spoil a guy."

She swatted at him lightly with a wooden spoon, a grin lighting her face. "Hush, you're the one who's going to be putting food on my table soon enough."

Malakai settled into a chair, noticing a stack of envelopes on the table—no doubt well-wishing cards from friends who'd heard the retirement news. His aunt set the platter down and ushered him to serve himself. "Eat up," she said brightly. "Got plenty."

The first bite of chicken delivered a burst of flavor—herby, tender, with a hint of tang. Malakai's shoulders relaxed as he savored it. Outside, the streetlights flickered to life, illuminating the quiet stretch of neighborhood. Soft shadows danced across Rochelle's kitchen walls, adding to the sense of intimate comfort.

When they both settled to eat, Rochelle dove into describing her day, arms flailing in dramatic emphasis. "I made the announcement at ten on the dot," she began, an impish twinkle in her eye. "You should've seen the looks on their faces. 'Rochelle, retiring? That can't be!' 'Who's going to run the diner, Miss Rochelle?'" She mimicked the gasps, pressing a hand to her chest.

Malakai nearly choked on a bite, muffling a laugh. "I can picture it now. Did the staff go into meltdown mode?"

She clicked her tongue. "A little. It was sweet, though. Some folks got teary-eyed, others bombarded me with frantic questions. It's like they can't imagine the diner without me. Bless 'em for their loyalty." She patted her chest. "Of course, I told them I have a family member stepping in."

He leaned forward, gripping his fork. "And… how'd that go over?"

A mischievous light gleamed in Rochelle's eyes. "Oh, honey, they lost their minds. 'Family? Rochelle has family? Who, where, how?'" She struck a dramatic pose. "I enjoyed every minute. I let them stew in it a bit before calmly stating you'll reveal yourself soon enough."

Malakai couldn't help but grin, imagining the chatter among the employees—especially *Aimee*, if she'd been there. How had she reacted? He forced himself to keep his expression neutral. "So, was Aimee around for that?"

Rochelle's lips curved knowingly. "Sure was, baby. Why? Looking for her reaction specifically?"

He feigned indifference, but heat creeped up his neck. "Just curious," he mumbled, lifting his glass of orange juice. The sweet tang melded well with the savory notes of dinner. "She's an important employee. Figured she might have a strong opinion."

Rochelle's pointed stare said she wasn't fooled, but she spared him further teasing for now. "She's definitely one of our best," she conceded. "All I'll say is she looked thoughtful. That girl cares deeply about the diner, so of course she's anxious about new ownership. But don't you worry." She reached out, patting his arm with maternal assurance. "Once she sees your heart's in the right place, she'll be on your side in a heartbeat."

Malakai swallowed, a gentle flutter at hearing that. "Thanks," he said quietly. He scooped another helping of rice onto his plate, determined to absorb every detail Rochelle offered. *So Aimee knows there's a secret family member,* he mused. *How's she imagining me?* Would she be suspicious? Intrigued? The thought tugged at him more than it should have.

As Rochelle moved on to share how various regulars had gasped, dropped napkins, and flailed in surprise, Malakai half-listened, half-lost in his own excitement. He felt a strange blend of anticipation and nerves. The quiet life he'd led, orchestrating everything from behind the scenes, was about to transform the moment he revealed himself. Sweetgum would see him for who he truly was—Rochelle's nephew, heir to the diner. Would they accept him, or would they balk at an outsider stepping in?

Eventually, Rochelle paused her storytelling to take another bite of chicken. Chewing contentedly, she shifted her gaze back to him. "So," she said after swallowing. "Did you message Mr. Germaine like you planned?"

Malakai nodded. "Yes, first thing this morning. Laid out a few new marketing angles, plus some potential menu additions. He responded within an hour, said he's ready to implement as soon as possible."

Rochelle beamed. "I can't wait to see how folks like the changes." Then her grin morphed into a theatrically stern expression. "You sure you want to keep playing sneaky-snake for another week?"

He tossed her a wry smile. "I do. I need that unfiltered insight—how the staff adjusts and how customers respond— before my presence changes the dynamic. I might pop in tomorrow as just another face, see how day one of the new suggestions goes." He rubbed the back of his neck, letting out a small breath. "I missed going in today. Felt strange not to watch the place in real time."

Rochelle's eyes glinted. "Or you missed a certain someone's face, too?"

He shot her a mock glare. "Stop reading my mind, Auntie." Despite himself, warmth flared in his chest at the thought of seeing Aimee again. It was a potent mix of curiosity and admiration, and maybe—just maybe—something more.

Rochelle gave a knowing laugh, lifting her glass in a small toast. "Here's to the next few days," she said. "May they be smooth. And to you, baby, for stepping up."

He lifted his own glass, the soft clink ringing in the dining room. "To new beginnings," he echoed, taking a sip. The tang of orange juice mingled with the savory flavors still dancing on his tongue, a reminder of how life's simplest pleasures could weave together unexpectedly.

They spent the rest of dinner in companionable conversation. Rochelle recounted more comedic highlights from her day —so-and-so nearly dropping their mug, or how two old friends had bickered over who might be the mysterious family member. Malakai chuckled, imagining the diner as a stage, each patron an eager actor in Rochelle's retirement drama.

Later, the plates emptied, and they cleared the table. Rochelle insisted he relax, but Malakai helped her anyway, hands deftly rinsing chicken grease and gravy from the dishes. The warm water and lavender-scented soap reminded him of the countless summers he'd spent here as a boy, handing her plates over the sink while she hummed a soulful tune. *Some things never change,* he mused gratefully.

When all was done, Rochelle patted his cheek affectionately. "You heading out, baby? Or do you want to stay for some dessert?"

Tempted though he was by potential sweets, Malakai's eyes

felt heavy from the day's tasks. "I better get going," he said gently. "I need an early start tomorrow."

She walked him to the door, the outside air gently chilling the night as he stepped onto the porch. The streetlamp in front of the house buzzed softly, casting shadows across the short walkway. Rochelle gave him one last hug, squeezing tight. "You take care, sugar," she murmured into his shoulder. "And remember, I'm rooting for you every step of the way."

He pulled back, smiling down at her. "Thanks, Aunt Rochelle. That means a lot." Turning to head down the steps, he flashed a final wave. "See you soon."

As he drove off, the hush of the darkened streets felt oddly comforting. It felt like Sweetgum was in that liminal space between old and new—Rochelle letting go of the diner's reins, and him about to take them up. His mind thrummed with the possibilities.

And somewhere in those possibilities, Aimee's face appeared again. *One more week, and she'll know who I really am,* he thought. Would she feel deceived by his secrecy? Or, with that bright passion she exuded, might she understand?

Gripping the steering wheel, Malakai pressed on the gas, guiding his car toward his apartment. Whatever the outcome, he vowed not to squander this chance to bring fresh life to Rochelle's Diner—and maybe, just maybe, to forge a deeper connection with the talented waitress whose eyes spoke volumes about her own unvoiced dreams.

CHAPTER NINE

$\mathcal{A}$imee exhaled into her cupped palms, relishing the brief warmth of her own breath against the biting morning chill as she pushed open the diner's front door. "I'm in," she announced quietly, stepping into the dim interior. It was a cold, dark hour—dawn still a mere hint on the horizon. *Four a.m. looks the same as midnight,* she mused, scanning the near-empty space. Sometimes she'd find a couple of night owls chattering over waffles in a far corner, but not today. This morning, the diner was just as sleepy as the sky.

"Aimee's here, bright and early!" a weary waitress behind the counter exclaimed, a shaky relief bleeding into her voice. She practically tore off her apron, letting it drop onto the counter with a sigh of utter resignation. "I was about to drop dead waiting for you." Without another word, she trudged toward the kitchen, presumably to wash up and head home.

Aimee moved behind the counter, blinking at the lonely apron with a suspicious grayish stain. Wrinkling her nose, she picked it up. "Yikes, that's going straight in the hamper," she muttered, catching a faint sour odor. She made her way into the short back corridor, where the overhead light buzzed softly in the early stillness.

The hallway was a simple space, painted in nondescript white. Two doors lined one side: one belonging to Rochelle—now absent from day-to-day operations—and the other to Mr. Germaine, the diner's manager. He typically didn't roll in until eight, so Aimee was doubly surprised to see a dim sliver of light beneath the door. She dropped the soiled apron in the hamper, pressing her lips together at the thought of how the diner's dynamic might change under the brand-new "mysterious" family member who'd taken over.

At least I'll have coffee, she consoled herself, turning to head back. A fresh cup would be the perfect companion to her early shift.

She'd barely taken two steps when a door creaked open behind her.

"Aimee. Hi, good morning."

She paused mid-stride and glanced over her shoulder. "Oh—Mr. Germaine," she said, eyebrows lifting. He looked as though he'd spent the night in that stuffy office, judging by the dark circles beneath his bloodshot eyes. Yet his suit remained neatly pressed, and his hair was immaculately cut. "I didn't expect to see you so soon."

He managed a tired half-smile, cradling a flask of steaming coffee. "You say surprising; I say unholy," he joked, voice rasping as though from too little sleep. "Anyway, can you come into my office for a minute? It's about something important."

Aimee's curiosity piqued instantly. "Sure," she replied, following him inside. Stacks of files teetered on the desk corners, casting angular shadows under the fluorescent lights. The heavy curtains were drawn, sealing out whatever faint glow filtered through the pre-dawn gloom. *Feels more like a secret bunker than a diner manager's office,* she thought, taking the rickety chair in front of his desk.

She tucked a loose strand of hair behind her ear. "So... how have things been, now that Rochelle's officially stepped back and her 'family member' is in charge?" She tried to keep her tone casual, though the entire staff still buzzed with questions about this unknown owner.

With a weary grunt, Mr. Germaine sank into his rolling chair, placing his coffee on a stack of folders. "Surprisingly good," he said, voice laced with unexpected enthusiasm. "I half-thought we'd crumble the minute Rochelle announced her retirement, but it's like whoever took over knows exactly what to do. It's almost as if Rochelle never left—minus her in-person scoldings, of course."

Aimee pressed her lips together, absorbing that bit of news. Rumors about Rochelle's "secret family" had run wild all yesterday, fueling speculation among customers and employees alike. "So, you've actually spoken to them? Met them?" she asked, leaning forward.

Mr. Germaine shook his head. "Not in person. Just emails. But those emails have enough detail to prove they know the business. And it's not just me—they had me gather input from the kitchen staff, the servers... you name it. I haven't seen such drive in a long time."

Her stomach fluttered with intrigue. Who *was* this person? She'd pictured some stern-looking uncle in a crisp suit or maybe a cousin from another state. "That's... interesting," she managed. *Weird, but interesting.* "So, is that why you asked me here? Some new directive from our mystery boss?"

A subtle spark lit Mr. Germaine's eyes, one she wasn't used to seeing. "Yes, actually. This directly involves you—and, well, Rochelle as well." He paused for dramatic effect. "They both insisted I ask if you'd be interested in developing a new soup recipe for the fall menu. You'd get a pay raise, full creative control... basically, you'd decide what goes into our weekly soup specials."

Aimee froze for a split second, heart hammering. "Wait—you're serious?" she breathed, a ripple of excitement coursing through her veins. She could almost feel her pulse thrumming in her fingertips. "They want me to—like, officially—create new recipes for the diner?"

Mr. Germaine nodded, rummaging through a messy pile of folders. "There's a contract. We'll finalize the details, but the gist is: more responsibility for you, more freedom to do what you do best, and more money. Win-win."

A stifled laugh of disbelief escaped her. She'd half-expected some routine shift change or extra hours. *But this?* It was an opportunity so perfect, it felt dreamlike. "I—I don't even know what to say," she stammered. "I'd love to do it. Absolutely."

She found herself thinking back to the conversation with Malakai—the "keep pushing yourself" vibe he'd offered. A twinge of warmth blended with the adrenaline surging in her chest. "I have a ton of ideas," she added quickly. "Pumpkin bisque, butternut squash soup, maybe a hearty chili or gumbo spin for fall. Oh!" She laughed, feeling borderline giddy. "I might be babbling. Sorry. It's just…this is huge."

"Babble away," Mr. Germaine replied, half-smiling at her enthusiasm. He flipped open his laptop, tapping briskly on the keyboard. "We'll print the updated contract now, so you can sign whenever. That cool?"

She placed a hand over her heart, inhaling deeply. "Yes, absolutely. Thank you." *And thank you, mysterious new owner,* she added silently.

~

By the time dawn broke fully over Sweetgum, Aimee was in her element. The diner slowly filled with the usual wave of hungry patrons, but she barely felt the weight of exhaustion that typically dogged her early shifts. Her mind raced through potential soup recipes, her steps light as she delivered plates of pancakes and refilled coffee cups with practiced flair. Even Mary, her somewhat apathetic coworker, seemed content to let Aimee handle most of the orders—likely because Aimee zipped around so quickly that Mary didn't need to lift a finger.

Sunlight spilled through the windows, painting golden bands across the tiled floor and illuminating the crisp autumn leaves on the sidewalk outside. Aimee hummed under her breath, though she wasn't sure if it was a random tune or sheer excitement. *A raise and creative freedom. Who would've guessed?*

Noon approached, bringing its typical lunch crowd. She was in the midst of wiping down the counter when a familiar ringing of the front door made her glance up. Her stomach fluttered instantly.

Malakai walked in, scanning the diner like he always did—quietly, thoughtfully. When his gaze landed on her, a subtle warmth lit his hazel eyes. He offered a faint nod, and she realized too late that she was openly staring. Caught, she flashed a tentative grin.

She tried not to think about how she'd told herself to steer clear of any complicated feelings. *He's a customer, Aims. Don't get carried away.* Still, the sheer comfort in his presence tugged at her heart in a way she couldn't ignore. She straightened, smoothing her apron, and approached him with a polite, "Good afternoon, Mr. Malakai. Perfect timing, as usual."

He lowered the menu he'd barely opened, raising an amused brow. "That's me. Right on cue." His lips curved in a gentle smile that made something fizz in her chest. "How've you been, Aimee?"

"Excellent, actually," she said, practically beaming. "I have news—big news. But maybe you'd like to order first?" She played at professionalism, though the excitement bubbled just beneath the surface.

Something amused danced in Malakai's expression. "Let's

hear your news first. I can decide on lunch in a minute." He tipped his chin toward the empty seat across from him. "Come on, indulge me."

Aimee hesitated—server etiquette usually demanded she stand. Yet, she'd seen Mary do it before, sliding into booths to chat with regulars. And Malakai certainly felt more friend than stranger these days. "I suppose…just for a second," she agreed softly, slipping into the seat. She pressed her notepad to her chest as if it could contain the pounding of her heart. Her instincts told her to keep her guard up, but something about him drew her in anyway.

"Okay," she breathed, "so… Rochelle retired yesterday." She paused, waiting to see how he'd react. His eyes flickered in interest, a slight crease forming between his brows. "She named some family member to take over—no one knows who. But they're already making changes. Like, guess who's been asked to develop a new soup recipe for the fall menu?" She bit her lip, her own excitement thrumming. "Yours truly. And it comes with a raise and basically creative freedom."

Malakai's face lit with a bright, genuine smile. He leaned in, hands clasped lightly on the table. "That's amazing, Aimee! Didn't I say you had the talent to make something bigger happen?" he asked with a teasing wink. "I'm genuinely thrilled for you."

Her chest soared at his words, cheeks warming under his unwavering gaze. "It all happened so fast," she admitted, recalling how just that morning she'd been complaining about the cold and dreading the early shift. "But apparently the new owner—or owners—think I can handle it." A soft laugh escaped her. "You know, you kind of hinted I should go for bigger stuff. It's like the universe listened to you."

Malakai's eyes shone. "I'm not surprised. Good work is always recognized eventually, right?" His tone was light, yet something in his voice carried a depth that made her pulse skip.

She tore her gaze from his, fiddling with the edge of her notepad. "Yeah, guess so. I'm, um, already brainstorming. Thinking pumpkin-squash soup, maybe a twist on chili…" Excitement rushed back in, loosening her tongue. "I want the diner to stand out while still keeping that homey vibe, you know? Can't scare off the locals."

"I get it," he said, nodding slowly. "Some people hate change, but it's amazing how small adjustments—like adding a signature soup—can spark new interest." His expression shifted, becoming almost intimate. "And I personally can't wait to see what you come up with. If you need a taste tester, count me in."

That last sentence hung in the air for a moment, making her heart flutter. He said it so casually, but she couldn't help reading more into it. *Stop overthinking,* she told herself. "You'd volunteer as guinea pig?" she teased, trying to keep her tone playful. "Caution: My test runs can get experimental. I wouldn't want to poison my best taster."

Malakai chuckled, resting one arm along the booth's back. It brought him a little closer, and Aimee caught a faint trace of his scent—clean and subtly spicy. "Poison me?" he echoed with mock horror. "No, no. I trust you implicitly. You haven't steered me wrong with any dishes so far."

Warmth flared in her cheeks again, and she was suddenly too aware of their proximity. Her eyes dropped to her notepad, which she clutched like a shield. "All right, then. Deal," she managed. "I'll rope you in for some top-secret soup tastings."

"Excellent," he said softly. The single word carried a thread of warmth that made her stomach flutter. *Focus,* she urged herself again, clearing her throat and sliding to the edge of the seat. She couldn't ignore that the diner was getting busier—someone would need a refill soon, and Mary was notoriously slow.

She rose from the booth, notepad at the ready. "So, *customer,* what can I get you for lunch?" she asked, injecting a playful lilt to keep things light.

Malakai arched a brow, as though mildly disappointed she was returning to "employee mode." But he humored her shift in tone. "Let's see," he mused, flipping open the menu he'd barely glanced at. "After hearing about your upcoming soup mania, I'm almost sad I can't taste it today. But I'll settle for the, uh, fish tacos. And maybe a side of the fries? The ones with that special seasoning you recommended last time?"

Aimee jotted it down, smiling. "Sure, fish tacos and seasoned fries. Got it." She gave him one last nod, her pulse still thrumming. "I'll be back with your drink in a moment."

She turned and headed toward the kitchen window, aware that her every step felt charged with an excitement she couldn't quite suppress. As she passed Mary, who was balancing an over-loaded tray, Aimee sensed her coworker's curious glance. She didn't need Mary's smirk to know it probably looked like she and Malakai were flirting.

But was that such a bad thing? A new wave of possibility lapped at Aimee's mind. Her morning had already upended her expectations—a random email from a faceless new owner, a brand-new opportunity to showcase her culinary dreams. So was it so strange to consider that maybe another door—one leading to a more personal connection—could also be opening?

Still, a tingle of caution prickled down her spine. She'd told herself she was done chasing illusions. *But this doesn't feel like chasing,* she reasoned, mentally pushing back. *It feels...natural.* The sense of contentment she found in Malakai's presence, the spark in his eyes when he encouraged her, the gentle undercur-rent of tension in their banter—it was all so different from her past heartbreaks. Safer yet thrilling at the same time.

Don't get ahead of yourself, she warned, sliding the order ticket to the cook. *Focus on the present.* She grabbed a glass, scooped ice, and filled it with water for Malakai, her heart still fluttering from that short conversation. The new soup project was plenty to be excited about without diving into uncertain emotional waters.

And yet...she couldn't help smiling as she carried the water back to Malakai's table. Because maybe—just maybe—the fresh wave of change rolling through the diner wouldn't only reshape her professional life. It might nudge her personal one, too, in a way she hadn't dared hope for before.

CHAPTER TEN

*A*unt Rochelle had mentioned dropping by the diner this afternoon to oversee some "business," and Malakai wished he could have picked another time to visit. He'd have preferred avoiding any overlap with her so he could quietly observe the operation—and yes, hopefully chat with Aimee without raising suspicions. But he wasn't about to miss seeing Aimee altogether, so if that meant sharing the place with Rochelle, so be it. *I just have to act normal,* he told himself for the umpteenth time, forcing his breathing to stay even.

He slipped into his usual booth near the window. Autumn light cast elongated shadows across the diner's tiled floor, adding a gentle coziness to the afternoon. He began drumming his thumbs lightly on the table, a steady, soft patter. *No slipping up,* he reminded himself. *They can't suspect anything.*

Out of habit, Malakai tapped his phone screen and pulled up an old email thread. It was a mundane conversation from months ago—just random business chatter, but a perfect cover whenever he needed to pretend he wasn't silently studying the diner. He flicked his gaze sideways. Out of the corner of his eye, he spotted Aimee waving from behind the counter, her smile bright enough to pierce the dull hush of midday. A warm spark flickered in his chest: *She really does light up a room.* A fleeting grin curved his lips in return, and she lifted a single finger in a quick I'll-be-right-there gesture before disappearing into the kitchen.

Always on the move, he thought, carefully schooling his features as he resumed scrolling. Ten minutes crawled by, with no sign of her. Restlessness fluttered in his stomach. Usually, he had the patience of a seasoned consultant, but waiting for Aimee tested him in a way few things did.

"Can I take your order?" a listless waitress asked, popping a wad of gum between her teeth. Her flat tone almost jolted him from his reverie.

He glanced up, shaking his head politely. "Not yet, thanks. Still deciding." The waitress bobbed her head, accepting his response without fuss, and shuffled over to a gray-haired gentleman seated in the middle of the diner.

Malakai stifled a slight smile—he recognized the posture of older folks squinting at small print. The man's menu was tilted at an odd angle, presumably to catch better light. Everything felt routine enough, except... *Why do I keep catching him glancing in my direction?* The man's gaze would flick over—just a moment— then return to the daily specials. *Probably nothing,* Malakai told himself, trying not to read too much into it.

Time slid by in short increments of anxious seconds. He risked another look, only to see the older man focusing squarely on his menu again—no hint of curiosity. *Maybe I imagined it.* Shrugging internally, Malakai returned his attention to the phone in his hand.

Suddenly, from the corner of his vision, he saw Rochelle stride into the dining area, balancing a steaming plate. Malakai's spine stiffened. *She's here already.* He forced his gaze down- ward as she breezed over to the gray-haired man. *So that's who she's bringing food to.* He risked a fleeting glance. The moment the dish landed, an unmistakable brightness sparked in both their faces. Warmth, familiarity—*Is she... seeing someone?* The notion struck him with unexpected force. Rochelle had never been the dating sort, as far as he knew. Yet the exchange between them held a quiet intimacy, stirring a pang of surprise —and a heavier dose of guilt. *I should be focusing on the diner's future,* he scolded himself, *not snooping into Rochelle's personal life.* But the curiosity lingered.

"I am so sorry I took so long."

Aimee's gentle voice cut through his swirling thoughts like a welcome knock on a half-open door. He glanced up, pulse quickening the moment her gaze met his. She appeared slightly breathless, her cheeks tinted with the soft flush of someone who'd been juggling tasks nonstop. His tension ebbed, replaced by a warmth low in his chest: *Thank God she's here.*

"It's fine," he said, lowering his tone so only she could hear. "I didn't mind waiting." He noticed the tray balanced on her arm, holding two white styrofoam cups. Steam curled in dainty spirals from the lids. *That smell...*

"Wait—you didn't order, right?" Aimee asked, setting the tray on his table. When he shook his head, she offered a grin. "Perfect. You're officially the ideal candidate to sample my latest masterpiece." A hint of playful triumph laced her voice.

He raised a brow, mind already pivoting away from any thoughts of Rochelle or the older gentleman. "Your latest masterpiece?" he echoed, letting a small smile slip free. "Are these... soups?" He caught the faint aroma of warm spices, something rich and savory that teased his senses.

Aimee nodded, excitement glowing in her eyes. "Yes! You promised to be my taste-tester, and I'm cashing in." She slid into the seat across from him—unusual for a server, but something about the way she did it felt perfectly natural. The movement tugged at Malakai's heart, an odd mix of tension and delight stirring in him. *Focus on the soup,* he told himself, though her presence made it tricky.

"These are my babies," she continued, pushing the cups forward. Steam drifted upward, wreathing them both in a cozy swirl of heat. "One is pumpkin squash, the other chili. I started them first thing this morning, hoping you'd be around to weigh in."

Malakai let out a soft exhale. *She did this partly for me?* The realization made his chest flutter. He lifted the first cup, the aroma enveloping him with earthy sweetness. "I'm honored," he said, lips curving. *I wish she knew how much this means.* He dipped a spoon into the pumpkin soup, closing his eyes for a brief second as warmth and flavor exploded on his tongue—a creamy mix of autumn comfort, balanced with just enough spice to intrigue. *Heavenly,* he thought.

He switched to the chili with a careful sip, savoring the tangy undertone and mild heat. The clash of flavors left him pleasantly torn. "You really nailed both," he said honestly, returning the pumpkin soup to his mouth for another quick sample. "If I had to choose... the pumpkin tastes like a genuine hug. Cozy, comforting. Chili's great, but the pumpkin has broader appeal."

Aimee's shoulders relaxed a fraction, relief washing over her expression. "That's what I was leaning toward, too," she admitted. "I love the chili, but some people can't handle spice, you know? And I wanted a soup that helps people feel at home."

He nodded, noticing the glow in her eyes. *She's doing more than cooking,* he realized. *She's infusing her heart into every dish.* "You definitely achieved that vibe," he said, letting the final vestiges of the soup's taste linger on his tongue. "And I won't complain if you eventually add the chili to the lineup. But if you're picking just one, I'd bet on pumpkin."

She toyed with a stray curl near her ear, a small quirk betraying her excitement. "Thanks for the feedback. I'm ready to pitch it to the manager. Guess I'll call it... 'Autumn Harvest

Pumpkin Soup' or something equally cozy." She paused, gaze flicking to his. "But you, Mr. Serious Taster—were you actually using some secret business skill back there? You looked intense."

Malakai's pulse jumped at how neatly she'd pinned him. "I was just… focusing," he hedged. "Food deserves all the attention we can give it." He immediately regretted the half-lie but forced a casual smile, hoping she wouldn't notice the slight edge in his tone.

Aimee stood, tray balanced against her hip. "Well, I appreciate your thorough approach," she said, her bright smile washing away his momentary anxiety. "I hope the rest of the customers love it as much as you do."

His heart did a small flip. "They will," he assured her, voice quieter now. "Trust me on that."

She nodded, stepping away from the booth. "Thanks, Malakai. Really. You've been a big help." Then she glided off, weaving between tables with a graceful efficiency that made it hard for him to drag his eyes away.

Focus. He inhaled, trying to steady himself. This was precisely why Aunt Rochelle had lectured him about flirting with a waitress under false pretenses. In truth, it was less about *flirting* and more about the natural connection that kept pulling him closer to Aimee. And that was the real danger—one he suspected Rochelle had already picked up on.

Stifling a resigned sigh, Malakai decided he should head out. He'd gleaned enough today—like how unstoppable Aimee's talent was. He left a tip on the table, a bit more generous than usual, then rose and headed for the door. *I can't stay all afternoon, especially with Rochelle somewhere in the building.* The thought of her catching him and Aimee chatting again tightened his chest.

Outside, the air carried a brisk chill, ushering in the deeper tang of autumn. He took one step toward his car, mind already replaying the spark in Aimee's eyes when she'd spoken about her soup.

"Look out!"

A startled shout broke his daze, forcing him to halt. He stared in confusion at a bright yellow fire hydrant, mere inches from his right knee. Realizing he'd nearly walked straight into it, he jerked back with a flush of embarrassment. He turned to see who'd warned him.

Aunt Rochelle stood there, arms folded over her chest, her expression hovering between exasperation and concern. "What is wrong with you?" she demanded, scanning him up and down. "Daydreaming so hard you can't see a giant hunk of metal?"

He swallowed, heart still hammering from the near collision. "I—uh—I had a lot on my mind," he stammered, pulling his hands from his pockets. "Didn't expect to run into you out here."

Rochelle pressed her lips together, faint lines etching deeper across her brow. "Doesn't matter. I know what I saw *inside*, Malakai." She arched a brow, her tone dropping. "You and Aimee, sitting together, having some *cozy* conversation about soup. *Very cozy.*"

An uneasy tightening clutched his gut. "We were just…taste-testing," he tried, lamely. "You know, she wanted an opinion—"

Rochelle sliced a hand through the air. "Don't sugarcoat it, boy. You're not just another customer asking for a refill, and we both know it. Aimee is under the impression that's all you are. Meanwhile, you're prepping to take over the diner and might change her entire world."

Malakai flinched at the bluntness. "I'm not trying to trick her," he insisted. *Or am I?* a guilty voice whispered inside him. "We just… get along. And I haven't lied—just omitted certain details." His stomach churned. "I planned to tell her soon."

Rochelle's stern gaze didn't waver. "You better. Because if she finds out by accident, it'll hurt her worse. Aimee's a trusting soul, baby. Don't you dare break that trust."

The weight of Rochelle's words sank in, pressing against

Malakai's chest. "I… I understand," he murmured, dropping his gaze to the sidewalk. "It's complicated."

She snorted softly, but her face softened a fraction. "Complicated or not, keep your priorities straight. If your interest in her is real, then be honest once the time's right. But if it's just idle flirting, you better cut it out. Clear?"

"Clear," he echoed in a low voice.

With that, Rochelle stepped back, exhaling. "I'll see you at dinner, baby," she added, turning away and marching back into the diner as quickly as she'd come.

Malakai stood there a moment longer, mind reeling. The crisp air nipped his face, but the real chill spread inside his rib cage. *She's right. This can't go on forever.* Eventually, Aimee would discover who he was and how closely her new soup initiative linked to his plans for the diner. A pinprick of dread surfaced. *What if she hates me for the deception?*

He let out a shaky breath, stepping off the curb and crossing the street. *Maybe I should come clean sooner than later.* But the thought of Aimee's reaction, how her trusting gaze might cloud with betrayal, twisted his stomach into knots.

"Just great," he muttered under his breath. *You wanted to help the diner, Malakai. Instead, you might end up hurting the person you respect most.* Tension pulled at his shoulders as he unlocked his car door.

Climbing inside, he glanced back at the diner's glowing windows. He pictured Aimee within those walls, brimming with passion for the craft she was finally allowed to explore. And him —supposedly her champion, though in truth he was the invisible boss. *Only one path forward,* he told himself. *Find the right moment to tell her. Pray she understands.*

Heart heavy, Malakai started the engine. The day had begun with anticipation, but now he felt stuck in a mire of conflicting obligations. As he drove off, the taste of Aimee's soup still lingered on his tongue—a bittersweet reminder that secrets, however noble, always carried a price.

CHAPTER ELEVEN

The Fall Harvest Festival was in full swing, flooding Sweetgum's town square with bright orange decorations, fragrant food stalls, and the easy camaraderie of friends enjoying autumn. Aimee couldn't help a small smile as she, Maia, and Alex ambled through the crowd, taking in every detail—from barrels overflowing with dried leaves to bales of hay scattered like makeshift seats around the square.

I love this time of year, she thought, lifting her phone to snap a quick photo of a towering pumpkin display. The crisp air carried a hint of woodsmoke, and the glow of festival lanterns began to emerge as afternoon edged toward twilight. If only this sense of magic could last forever.

They ended up near a bustling booth offering fresh brownies and hot coffee samples. Aimee nibbled a small square of fudgy chocolate, half-listening as Maia replayed a rom-com plotline in far too much detail. The line for coffee wound halfway around the stand, but the aroma of freshly brewed beans—and the sight of happy festivalgoers cradling steaming mugs—made it worth the wait.

"...and then at the end," Maia was saying, cheeks tinted with excitement, "he just wraps her up and starts showering her cheek with kisses. I swear, it'd be the perfect pick for tomorrow's movie screening."

Alex offered a fond, if slightly skeptical, grin. "It's popular, sure, but the festival committee might go with something more family-friendly."

Aimee let out a wry laugh, brushing a few stray bangs from her face. "Maia, you won't take logic from anyone. You just want a romantic movie because you're hopelessly in love." She feigned a gag, then winked to show she was only teasing. "If I had to bet, they'll pick a classic—safe for kids, easy to set up. Something sweet but not so sappy."

Maia let out a mock sigh. "You're raining on my parade. Isn't she, Alex?" She snuggled closer to him, pulling her paper bag of mini candied apples protectively against her side. The sweet smell of caramel coated the already autumn-scented air.

He just chuckled. "I'm Switzerland here," he said lightly, "though I wouldn't object to cuddling during a cheesy romance."

Aimee snorted, genuinely pleased at how content Maia and Alex looked together. They'd toned down their more demonstrative affection around her—a gesture she appreciated, even if she insisted she was fine. A tiny flutter of longing ignited in her thoughts, but she swiftly buried it beneath the day's warmth. She had no reason to feel lonely, not when the festival glowed with life and promise.

"So," Alex said, turning a curious eye on Aimee, "didn't you mention a new guy at the diner? I remember you saying he's come in a couple of times—didn't he give you feedback on that fall soup you made?"

"Oh, yes!" Maia chimed, her eyes lighting up with mischief. She let out a small squeal that made Aimee blush. "The one who coincidentally shows up during your shifts. That same one who's handsome, right?"

Aimee pinched Maia's arm lightly, though her cheeks

warmed. "Stop it," she mumbled. "He's just another customer. Nice, sure, but that doesn't mean anything."

Maia laughed. "You sound exactly like I did before I started dating Alex." She pressed a playful kiss to Alex's shoulder, prompting an affectionate smile from him. Overhead, street-lamps sparked to life, draping the square in a gentle glow.

Aimee held up a finger as if scolding. "This is different. I don't even know Malakai that well. He's just some random out-of-towner." She tried to sound casual but felt a subtle twist in her chest. The truth was, he wasn't *just* a random guy. He'd been fueling her confidence about her cooking, and that had felt so… good.

"Wasn't I 'some random guy' too?" Alex teased, arching a brow.

"Yeah, but that's—" She waved a hand dismissively, pretending irritation. "Shush. Let's order."

The coffee booth line finally thinned, so the trio claimed their steaming cups. As they wandered away, the festival's evening vibe swelled: bright lights, vibrant music, and families drifting among carnival games and craft stalls.

Aimee took a careful sip of her coffee, letting the comforting aroma anchor her swirling thoughts. "All right, folks," she announced, "I only have about an hour before I have to head back for the diner meeting. Let's figure out what we're doing next."

Maia spotted a lively corner where people were cheering around a makeshift game labeled *Shovel the Leaves*. She pointed with wide-eyed excitement. "Want to watch that for a bit, or maybe join in?"

Aimee shrugged with a smile. "Sure, why not?"

They meandered over, exchanging laughs and commentary as they observed festival-goers valiantly scooping massive piles of leaves into barrels. Bright laughter and the crunch of dried foliage merged into a soundtrack of autumn joy. Yet Aimee couldn't fully push aside the flutter of nerves: *Tonight's the diner meeting. We're actually meeting the new owner.* Her stomach did a tiny somersault. *Whoever he is,* she thought, glancing at her watch.

Eventually, the time came for her to part ways with Maia and Alex. She exchanged swift hugs. "I hate to dash off," she said regretfully, "but if I'm late, Mary will never let me hear the end of it."

Maia gave her a mischievous grin. "Go, go! We'll fill you in on anything fun you miss."

Aimee waved goodbye and headed toward Main Street at a brisk pace. Unfortunately, weaving through festival crowds cost her precious minutes. By the time she neared the diner, she was a solid ten minutes behind schedule. She jogged the last stretch, cheeks flush from the chill air and the rush to arrive.

"Sorry I'm late!" she called upon bursting through the doors, spotting a circle of chairs arranged near the front. Half the tables had been shoved aside, opening the space for this impromptu gathering. Familiar faces dotted the ring of seats— the waitresses, cooks, and other staff from both morning and night shifts. At the center stood Rochelle, wearing a bright orange dress with a fresh blue ribbon pinned to the fabric.

Rochelle flashed a gracious smile. "No worries," she said gently. "I was pretty late myself. Go ahead and sit, dear. Let's get started."

Wrestling off her jacket, Aimee slipped into an empty seat next to Mary. Around her, staff members fidgeted with a shared excitement—some looking giddy, others wearing guarded skepticism. *Finally,* Aimee thought, *we'll learn who's been calling the shots.* Her stomach churned with both hope and uncertainty. *Could it be some distant relative with no clue how diners work, or someone who's about to turn our routines upside-down?*

Rochelle clasped her hands in front of her. "As you know, I officially retired last week. With that, I mentioned a family member would be stepping in as the diner's new owner." That single statement reignited a low wave of murmurs. Folks shifted in their seats, exchanging glances. Some were just plain curious, while others seemed skeptical after the hush-hush lead-up.

Aimee's fingers tightened around the hem of her sweater. *A male relative,* she noted from previous hints. *But who?* She forced a calm breath, ignoring Mary's playful nudge.

"In the past week," Rochelle continued, "most of you have received emails from our new head in charge. But no one's met him—at least not officially."

A ripple of anxious energy passed around the circle. The older cook voiced a grumble about "long-drawn-out drama," while one of the younger servers giggled nervously. Aimee fiddled with a loose thread on her seat cushion, her mind spinning. *We might as well enjoy the show,* she told herself, *and hope for the best.*

Rochelle disappeared around the counter for a moment, leaving the staff in a crescendo of chatter. Aimee leaned to Mary and whispered, "We're finally about to see this mystery man." Mary just rolled her eyes good-naturedly, but even she looked intrigued.

When Rochelle returned, she had a tall figure at her side, guiding him into view. Aimee's eyes darted to his forest green sweater first—*and then her heart slammed to a halt.*

Malakai.

He offered a polite, almost practiced smile, his confidence radiating differently than it did when he walked into the diner as a "customer." Rochelle glowed with pride. "Everyone," she announced, "this is my nephew—the new owner of our lovely little diner."

Polite applause rippled through the group. But Aimee sat motionless, the clapping a distant roar in her ears. *Nephew? New owner?* Shock tumbled through her thoughts in a dizzying wave. He was behind the emails. He was the one making decisions about my soup. She felt a sudden rush of confusion, anger, and an ache so deep it nearly knocked the breath from her. *He's... not who I thought he was.*

She caught a glimpse of Malakai scanning the crowd. His gaze collided with hers, and a spark of guilt—or was it regret?—flickered in his expression. The rest of the staff cheered, but Aimee stayed frozen. A thousand questions pressed at her: *How could he hide this? Why did he pretend to be just another friendly stranger?*

Malakai cleared his throat, launching into a short speech about his plans for the diner, praising Rochelle's legacy. The staff listened with a mix of curiosity and cautious optimism. Some fired off quick questions: "Will we get new equipment?" "What about the specials?" The older cook nodded along approvingly when Malakai referenced tradition.

He's so poised, she thought bitterly, a knot twisting in her belly. *Must be nice, waltzing in here with the perfect words, after leading me on.* Except... had he led her on? She didn't even know. They weren't in a relationship, but they'd built a rapport, a closeness she'd valued. The sting of betrayal gripped her throat. *I told him personal stuff. He encouraged me. Was that all part of the ruse?*

When his speech wrapped up, the staff erupted into a louder round of applause. Aimee tried to lift her hands, but she couldn't clap. Her palms felt clammy, her heart pounding. Blood roared in her ears.

As the meeting eased into casual chatter, Malakai shifted, clearly intending to approach her. Panic flared. She needed air. She needed not to break down in front of her coworkers. *I have to get out of here.* Without waiting, she slipped sideways out of the circle, making for the side door.

The cool night air hit her like a slap. She stumbled a few steps down the alley, hugging her arms across her chest. Her eyes prickled with tears she refused to let fall. *It's not like we were ever dating. I have no right to feel so heartbroken.* But the ache in her chest didn't care about logic.

A moment later, footsteps crunched on gravel behind her. She tensed, spinning around to see Malakai silhouetted in the dim glow of a nearby lamp. The anguished look on his face nearly shattered her composure.

"Aimee," he murmured, voice thick with remorse. "I... I'm so sorry."

She stared at him, heart pounding. Everything she'd felt—the slight flutter of hope, the pride in showing him her soup, the sense that maybe, just maybe, she'd found someone to believe in her—twisted into a raw ache. "So you're Rochelle's nephew," she said hoarsely, forcing the words out. "You've known this whole time."

He took a step closer. "Yes. I had to keep it quiet so I could see how the diner worked from a true customer's perspective. I never wanted to hurt you."

Her anger flared. She clutched her elbows tighter, memories of their easy conversations flickering like cruel flashes. "But you did hurt me. All those times you asked about my soup, or about the menu, or about my job... You let me believe you were just some random guy." Her voice wavered dangerously, tears threatening to spill. "Why couldn't you just tell me the truth once you realized I was trusting you?"

He looked devastated, shoulders sagging. "Aimee, I wanted to—but the moment I started to, I realized how it would look: like I was using you for intel or... or playing with your feelings. I didn't know how to fix it." He paused, desperation in his voice. "I *never* faked my admiration for your cooking. That was always real."

She swallowed hard, tears burning behind her eyes. "You know what hurts the most? That I opened up—about my ideas, my excitement. I told you I was so happy to finally have a chance with the new owner's blessing, and you just... played along. You stood there and pretended not to know. Like it was some big joke."

He reached out a trembling hand but stopped inches from her arm, unsure if she'd accept it. "It wasn't a joke," he insisted softly. "When you told me you got that soup opportunity, I—I was proud. I wanted you to have it. I swear, Aimee."

She squeezed her eyes shut, fighting the betrayal throbbing in her chest. *We weren't together. He never promised me anything.* But the blow to her trust stung like heartbreak. *Why does it hurt this much?*

Slowly, she opened her eyes. His gaze bore into hers, pleading for understanding. Part of her wanted to run into the diner, away from the swirling chaos in her mind. But she forced herself to stand firm, voice trembling. "If you cared," she whispered, "if you *really* cared, you would've told me. Or at least tried to. We... we talked about so many things, Malakai. You knew how important being honest and real is to me. How could you...?"

He bowed his head, tension radiating off him. "I messed up," he admitted, voice rough. "I was in too deep before I realized how you might feel. Then I was afraid I'd lose your trust completely if I confessed too late."

She gave a bitter laugh, tears finally spilling over. "Well, you've definitely lost it now." Her voice cracked, and she hated how vulnerable she sounded. They were never anything—yet it felt as though her heart had been wrenched out. "Just go back inside. Let's not make this any more humiliating for me than it already is."

"Aimee—"

She backed up a step, pressing a shaky palm against the cold brick wall. "Please," she said, tears shining on her cheeks. "Not now. I—I can't do this right now. I need to breathe. I need time."

He looked like he wanted to argue, but ultimately, he just nodded, sorrow etched into every line of his expression. She turned, her stomach twisting, and hastened toward the main street. Even though she was walking away from her job, from the diner staff who might see her meltdown, she couldn't bear staying in that alley with him another second.

As soon as she rounded the corner, she sank against the side of another building, choking back a sob. The festival lights glowed in the distance, laughter and music mocking her heartbreak. *This is ridiculous,* she scolded herself. *We weren't a couple.* But the betrayal stung all the same. She'd let herself hope—hope that maybe her life could contain a little romance, a partnership in both cooking and genuine connection. The memory of Malakai praising her soup replayed in her head, now tainted with the knowledge that he had all the power the whole time.

She raised a trembling hand to her forehead, breath coming in shaky gasps. *He never explicitly lied about feelings,* she reminded herself. *He's still just my boss.* But no logic could soothe the twist of pain in her chest. The illusions she'd begun to nurture had crashed down like a fragile display of fine china.

Slowly, she steadied her breathing. The quiet hush of evening settled around her. She knew she couldn't stand there forever, so she forced herself upright, wiping tears with the back of her hand. *I'll have to face him eventually.* But for now, she had to deal with her swirling emotions in private.

She took a step back toward the festival noise, letting the colorful lights blur through her still-wet lashes. *Why,* she thought as her heart gave one more painful squeeze, *did it have to be him who made me hope again?* She shivered against the chilly air, hugging herself for comfort. No easy answers came, and the realization only deepened the ache in her chest.

CHAPTER TWELVE

Malakai stayed where he was for a long moment after Aimee slipped back inside, the back door's gentle thud echoing in the quiet alley. In the distance, festival lights still glowed over the rooftops, a bittersweet reminder of how quickly a celebratory mood could vanish.

I should've told her sooner, he thought, the words looping in his mind like an unrelenting drumbeat. He took a slow breath, forcing his shoulders back. Inside that diner stood the woman whose eyes had brimmed with a hurt he'd never intended to cause—and he had to face it.

Bracing himself, he stepped through the rear entrance. By the time he entered the main dining area, most of the staff had drifted into their usual routines or gathered in low-voiced clusters to discuss the big news. A handful lingered near the windows, curiosity and hesitant excitement etched on their faces as he walked by. *I should be out here exuding confidence as the new owner,* he thought. *But all I want is to apologize to one person.*

He forced a tight nod at two cooks whispering behind raised hands. Their stares spoke of confusion—maybe even mild suspicion. He debated giving a quick, public apology for any confusion, but what he wanted most was to see Aimee. *Nothing else matters until I fix this,* he told himself, scanning the room.

There—near the front counter, Aimee stood answering a question from a veteran waitress. The older woman leaned in, and Aimee replied with polite, measured words. The tension in Aimee's jaw betrayed her. He could sense she was trying to appear calm, but the flicker of hurt in her eyes when she blinked told him she was fighting more emotion than she could show.

She's in pain. The realization twisted his gut with a sharper intensity than he'd expected. *And it's because of me.* He hated himself for letting it get to this. If only he'd found a way to be honest before unveiling it to the entire staff.

He wove around a couple of employees who bustled over to congratulate him, forcing an absent smile. Their words—"Congrats, sir!" and "We're so excited for you!"—bounced off him. *I barely know how to respond,* he admitted to himself. He gave polite, short answers and kept moving, eyes locked on Aimee's figure in the distance.

Just as he was about to approach her, a short-order cook intercepted him, brandishing a notepad and beaming. "Hey, boss, so I've got these ideas for daily specials. I'd love your thoughts!" The cook's enthusiasm would normally fill him with pride, but Malakai's mind was elsewhere. He mustered a courteous nod, skimming the scribbled list. Meanwhile, Aimee was fielding yet another question from someone else. *She's so close,* he thought, a throbbing impatience coiled in his chest. *I need just a moment with her.*

He did his best to listen to the cook's pitch—something about rotating burger toppings and a new Friday fish fry—nodding at intervals. But the entire time, he felt Aimee's presence like a gravitational pull. Each second that passed ratcheted his anxiety higher. *She'll walk away, or she'll leave,* he fretted.

Eventually, the cook thanked him for listening and bustled off, satisfied with his new boss's minimal encouragement.

Malakai exhaled in relief, pivoting toward Aimee again—only to see Aunt Rochelle waving him over from a corner booth with that familiar "don't leave me hanging" look.

Aunt Rochelle. Right. He couldn't ignore her. He owed everything to her, and part of him understood she'd want updates. But frustration built. *This is the last thing I want right now, but I can't blow her off.*

He forced himself to cross the diner floor, weaving between staffers who nodded respectfully, a swirl of compliments and well-wishes trailing after him. With each step, he caught a glimpse of Aimee behind the counter, shoulders rigid. She refused to glance his way, focusing on wiping down surfaces that didn't really need it.

When he reached Rochelle, she was just murmuring a goodbye to another staff member. Once alone, she turned to him, gaze sharp. "How'd it go, baby?" she asked quietly, motioning for him to sit across from her. She was half-turned in the booth, her posture showing equal parts concern and exasperation.

Malakai stayed standing, arms tensed at his sides. "She's… upset," he said in a low voice, eyes flicking toward the front again. "You were right. I should've told her sooner. I didn't realize she'd feel so strongly." *I didn't realize I'd feel this strongly,* he added silently.

Rochelle's stern look softened a bit. "Boy, a heart as big as Aimee's is bound to feel betrayed," she said, shaking her head. "All you can do now is give her some air. Don't crowd her. Let her decide if and when she's ready to hear more."

He nodded grimly, his gut churning. The possibility of her never forgiving him loomed like a storm cloud. Before he could respond, Rochelle spotted another staff member motioning for her attention and rose to greet them, slipping away in a swish of her bright dress.

Left alone in the booth for a second, Malakai rubbed the

back of his neck, adrenaline thrumming in his veins. *I can't just vanish without acknowledging her.* Even if she wanted space, he couldn't leave her with the impression that he was uncaring or oblivious.

Turning, he found her again—*still* behind the counter, wiping and re-wiping the same stretch of polished formica. Another waitress joined her briefly, likely asking if Aimee needed help. Aimee shook her head, forcing a polite smile that didn't reach her eyes. She was obviously trying to mask her turmoil with busywork.

I have to say something. A simple apology, at least. Steeling himself, he crossed the diner. The overhead lights felt harsher, each step a reminder that every staff member present could be watching. But he didn't care. He slowed as he approached, calling her name softly. "Aimee?"

She turned, startled. For an instant, the hurt in her eyes was painfully clear—before she suppressed it, bracing her hands on the counter. "Malakai," she said, her tone holding a guarded edge.

He swallowed the tightness in his throat, lowering his voice so only she could hear. "I won't push you," he began, hands fidgeting at his sides. "But I need you to know—I'm not ignoring this. I get it, I messed up, and I need to earn your trust back."

Her eyes flickered with conflicting emotions, and for half a heartbeat, she looked on the verge of tears. Then she locked her jaw, inhaled, and nodded stiffly. "Yes. You do," she agreed, voice wavering just enough to reveal her pain.

The simple acknowledgement hit him like a punch. *She's shutting me out, but at least she's being honest,* he told himself. He forced a swallow. "All right," he murmured. "If you need space, I respect that. But if there's anything—"

She exhaled shakily, cutting him off with a slight shake of her head. "Thank you," she managed. She glanced away, dismissing him without another word, her body language screaming that she wasn't ready for further conversation.

Malakai's chest felt hollow, but he made himself step back. She needed room to process, and no matter how strong his urge was to lay everything out—how he'd never intended to fool her or manipulate her—he had to let her lead. *She's worth waiting for,* a voice inside him affirmed.

He offered a curt nod, then turned on his heel. One of the younger cooks caught him mid-departure, shaking his hand and congratulating him with genuine warmth. Malakai went through the motions, returning the handshake, faking a grateful smile. But his mind was trapped in the swirl of heartbreak etched on Aimee's face.

At last, he slipped toward the diner's front exit. He spared one final glance over his shoulder, hoping beyond hope she might be looking his way. Their eyes met for a flicker of a second. She quickly turned, resuming her conversation with Mary. *The hurt is still there,* he thought, guilt pressing heavily at his ribs. *She's trying so hard to act normal, and it's tearing me up inside.*

Outside, the late-evening air felt colder than before. A brisk wind rustled the leaves along Main Street, carrying the distant hum of festival celebrations. What a difference from just a few hours ago, when he'd arrived brimming with quiet excitement about finally stepping into the role of diner owner. Now the only thing he felt was the raw sting of regret.

He paused on the sidewalk, letting the swirl of emotions settle. The question beat in his mind: *How do I make this right?* Aimee's talent had drawn him in, but her spirit and warmth had kept him coming back. He never meant to betray her trust—yet that was precisely what he'd done.

Steadying himself, he inhaled the scent of fallen leaves. *I can't leave it like this.* One step at a time, though. She needed breathing room before he apologized properly, away from prying eyes and rushed schedules.

With that resolve anchoring him, he headed down the dimly lit block toward his car. A swirl of crisp autumn wind tugged at his jacket, and he imagined Aimee's eyes in that final moment—hurt, disappointed, closed off. His heart clenched. *I'll fix this*, he vowed silently. *If she'll let me. Whatever it takes, I'll make amends.*

But deep in the pit of his stomach, a gnawing fear whispered: *What if it's already too late?*

CHAPTER THIRTEEN

*K*nock. *Knock. Knock. Knock. Knock...*
Aimee's fist connected with Maia's door again, each rap landing louder and more urgent than the last. The chill night air clung to her coat, sending a prickle down her spine each time she shifted. *Please open up,* she silently begged, her heart thumping from both the cold and the roiling emotions in her chest. She knew it was late—Maia might be drifting off with a good book or half-asleep after the festival. *But this can't wait.*

At last, the gold lock clicked. The door cracked open to reveal Maia, her eyes blinking away the haze of near-sleep. Clad in pajamas and a bright pink bonnet, she looked cozy and taken by surprise.

"Aimee?" Maia's eyebrows shot up, alarm shadowing her features when she noticed Aimee's tense posture. "Hey, are you okay?"

"Can we talk?" Aimee asked in a hushed, trembling voice. She forced herself to meet Maia's concerned gaze. *If she doesn't let me in, I might break down on her doorstep.*

"Of course." Maia instantly stepped aside, ushering her in.

The lingering warmth of Maia's home enveloped Aimee, a stark contrast to the crisp darkness outside.

MINUTES LATER, Aimee found herself perched on the edge of Maia's plush sofa, hugging her knees tight, as Maia poured them both a generous glass of red wine. The soft clink of glass on bottle seemed to echo in the quiet living room, a surprisingly tense sound that set Aimee's nerves on edge. She drummed her fingers on her thigh, fidgeting with a loose thread on her coat's seam.

"Okay," Maia said, settling cross-legged on a cushion opposite Aimee. She handed over one of the wine glasses. "I heard something about Malakai being the world's biggest liar, from your text. I'm guessing you saw him tonight?" She took a small sip, her face lined with worry.

Aimee let out a shaky breath, bracing for the wave of anger and betrayal that flared every time she replayed the evening. "Yes." She swallowed, her voice tight. "The staff meeting at the diner? The one where we were supposed to meet the new owner?"

Maia nodded slowly, her expression growing more puzzled by the second. "Right...?"

A spark of hurt flared in Aimee's chest, renewing the sting. "He *is* the owner, Maia," she said, voice quivering with frustration. "He's Rochelle's 'secret family'—her nephew. He's been under cover all this time, pretending to be some random nice customer who'd show up whenever I worked."

She dragged a trembling hand through her curls, her anger bolstered by fresh embarrassment. "All those compliments, all that so-called interest in me—turns out it was just part of his hidden mission to watch the diner and see how we run things." Her throat tightened painfully as she grabbed the glass of wine

Maia had set out. Nearly sloshing its contents, she raised it to her lips and gulped. "I feel like such a fool."

"Wait, what?" Maia's mouth fell open in stunned disbelief. She took a bigger swallow of her own wine, blinking as though trying to piece together Aimee's words. "So he was… basically an undercover boss?"

Aimee nodded, biting down on her lower lip. "That's exactly what he was. Never once told me who he really was. He let me think everything was just a lucky friendship or I don't even know what. For weeks." She released a bitter scoff, swirling her wine in short, angry circles. "Apparently, it was all part of his plan. Once he'd gleaned enough, he'd step forward as the new owner. And me? I was just convenient—this naive waitress who spilled her heart about cooking and the diner's daily grind."

Maia's lips pressed together in a thin line. "That's… a lot to swallow," she said after a moment, anger kindling in her eyes. "But are you sure it was all fake? Did he actually say, 'I only cared about the business side' or anything like that?"

Aimee gulped back the harsh sting of tears, a swirl of heartbreak tightening in her chest. "He didn't have to say it," she muttered, her voice raw. "He admitted he had reasons for hiding his identity—he wanted to see the 'real' diner. But how can I believe anything else he said about me—my cooking, my ideas—was genuine? If he can lie about who he is so easily, how can I trust any of it was real?"

Maia exhaled sharply, sympathy flickering in her gaze. "I'm not defending him," she said, voice carefully calm. "But maybe it's worth hearing his side, you know? Because if he truly wanted to sabotage you, he wouldn't have encouraged you to pitch new recipes. Right?"

Aimee's shoulders slumped, her anger tangling with a sense of longing she despised. She slouched back, feeling drained. "He looked guilty tonight, like he hated admitting everything. And afterward, he tried to talk to me outside… but I was too angry and embarrassed to really listen." She took another shaky sip of wine, letting the warmth soothe her for a moment. "I just can't get past that initial betrayal. This whole time, I was opening up to him about my goals, my life. And he was basically my boss in disguise."

Maia inched closer, resting a comforting hand on Aimee's shoulder. "Anyone would feel shocked and hurt," she said gently. "But if there's guilt in his eyes, maybe he regrets how it all played out. Maybe his feelings were real—just overshadowed by this plan to hide his identity."

Aimee's heart clenched. She pictured Malakai's eyes as he'd apologized earlier in the alley, raw regret shining through. Even recalling it now made her chest tighten with conflicting emotions. "Why does it have to be so complicated?" she whispered. "We weren't even dating. I shouldn't feel so... broken over this."

Maia's expression softened even more. "Sometimes it hurts because you let yourself hope for something," she said gently, giving Aimee's shoulder a light squeeze. "That alone can be painful when trust is broken."

For a moment, Aimee couldn't form words. She cast her gaze around Maia's living room—soft lamplight, warm cushions, a sense of serenity that felt at odds with the storm in her mind. "I thought maybe I'd found someone who believed in me," she murmured, voice trembling. "I'd put romance on the back burner, but it was still nice, you know? Feeling seen. Feeling like... maybe there was a connection."

Maia's eyes shone with sympathy. "It's not foolish to let yourself hope," she said gently. "Love—any form of connection —comes with risks."

Aimee swallowed around the tightness in her throat, tears threatening to spill. "Well, that hope's gone now," she managed, half-laughing to mask her hurt. "He had a plan, and I was just the easiest way to see the diner from an insider's perspective. Nothing more."

Maia slid an arm around Aimee's shoulders, pulling her into a comforting side hug. Aimee closed her eyes, absorbing the quiet strength of her best friend's presence. *Thank God for Maia,* she thought, letting a teardrop slip onto the shoulder of Maia's pajama top.

They sipped wine in silence for a moment, the TV playing softly in the background. Aimee's mind reeled with images of Malakai praising her soup, gently nudging her to believe in her skills. *Was any of it real?* The question throbbed like a bruise. He hadn't denied his admiration, but *he never told me the truth,* her mind insisted.

Eventually, Maia cleared her throat. "You're off the next couple of days, right?" she asked, grabbing the TV remote from a nearby cushion.

"Yes," Aimee said, her voice still subdued. "Thank goodness I'm not stuck facing him at work."

"Then let's distract you," Maia declared, turning on the TV with an air of determination. "Let's find some big, dumb action flick that's too loud and silly for you to think about anything else."

Aimee mustered a shaky laugh, nodding. "Yes, please," she said, feeling the tension begin to uncoil. *Maybe mindless explosions and bad dialogue are exactly what I need right now.*

The screen lit up, revealing a movie that wasted no time launching into chase scenes and over-the-top stunts. For the next two hours, they sipped their wine, exchanging occasional commentary about how ridiculous the plot was. Yet, within that sheer absurdity, Aimee found a measure of calm. *I can't fix how I feel tonight,* she realized, *but at least I'm not facing it alone.*

~

EARLY THE FOLLOWING DAY, Aimee accompanied Maia to a scheduled gown fitting at the dress shop. Stepping inside felt akin to crossing into another world. Plush carpeting hushed their footsteps, mannequins draped in shimmering ivory flanked them, and the fragrance of lavender and freshly pressed linen merged in a serene hush. *A far cry from last night's turmoil,* Aimee thought, inhaling the soothing scent.

Maia changed into her partially completed gown with the tailor's help, disappearing behind a curtain. When she emerged, Aimee's breath caught. The gown's silken layers fell around Maia in delicate folds, capturing the morning light with an almost magical glow.

"Wow," Aimee breathed, the word hardly enough to encompass how radiant her friend looked. Despite the ache still lodged in her own chest, seeing Maia beam in that dress filled Aimee with genuine joy.

"I'm just… in love with it," Maia whispered, looking at herself in the mirror with shining eyes.

Terrence, the co-owner and tailor, stood nearby with a measuring tape draped around his neck. "We'll alter the sleeves and add subtle beading," he explained. "You'll be picture-perfect."

Aimee carefully snapped a few photos from different angles so Maia could send them to Alex. The glow on Maia's face was unmistakable. "If Alex sees you like this," Aimee teased softly, "he's going to melt before the wedding even starts."

Maia chuckled, a rosy flush on her cheeks. "He'd better be strong enough to stand at the altar," she joked. "Is it bad luck to send him these pictures?"

Terrence waved off her concern with a knowing smile. "You're not in the full bridal ensemble yet, so the tradition's intact."

Aimee helped Maia navigate the soft folds of the dress as she prepared to change back. *So this is what real love looks like—abso-*

lute faith in each other, she thought. The corners of her lips tightened as her mind slipped to Malakai again. She *wanted* to believe in him, but how could she, after all those secrets?

Once Maia changed into her regular clothes, they thanked Terrence and stepped into the main showroom. Each mannequin wore a distinct style of gown, some lavish, some understated. It felt like a palace of romance and promise, at odds with Aimee's current heartbreak.

Yet for the brief moment, she let herself be pulled into Maia's giddy excitement. They exchanged grateful goodbyes with Terrence and ventured outside, where the midday sun cast warm, forgiving rays. The hum of Sweetgum's bustle returned, a welcome sign of normalcy.

Maia slipped an arm through Aimee's, beaming. "That was wonderful," she sighed, her voice soft with contentment. "Thanks for coming, Aims. I know you have your own stuff going on."

Aimee forced a smile, though the memory of last night still pressed heavily at the corners of her mind. "I wouldn't miss it for anything. Seeing you that happy… it helps."

Maia gave her arm a gentle squeeze. For a moment, they strolled in easy silence, the clang of a nearby construction site and the chatter from a passing group of shoppers weaving into the background noise. *Life goes on,* Aimee told herself, *even when your heart's bruised.*

A swirl of leaves skittered across the sidewalk, and Aimee caught the faintest hint of cinnamon drifting from a nearby café. Her stomach lurched at the recollection that Malakai used to mention his love for fall flavors. She clenched her jaw, trying not to let the memory sour the crisp day. *I can't keep letting him invade my thoughts.*

Maia turned, studying Aimee's drawn expression. "You know," she said gently, "if you decide you want to hear Malakai out, I'd stand behind you. If you decide otherwise, I'll still stand behind you. No matter what."

For a second, the sincerity in her friend's voice nearly made tears swell in Aimee's eyes again. She gave Maia's arm a grateful squeeze in return. "Thank you," she whispered. "I'm still figuring out what I want—whether I can trust him or not."

Maia nodded, compassion softening her features. "Take your time. You're allowed to guard your heart, but sometimes letting someone explain can bring peace, even if you don't end up trusting them again."

Aimee's chest constricted at the notion of giving Malakai a chance to defend himself. A part of her craved an honest explanation—why he'd done it, how he truly felt—yet another part insisted it was safer to slam that door shut. She inhaled, letting the autumn air fill her lungs, the mild sunshine momentarily comforting. *I can't decide now*, she admitted to herself.

They continued down Main Street, the light breeze ruffling Maia's hair and tugging at the sleeve of Aimee's jacket. A swirl of conversation from a nearby coffee shop reminded Aimee of simpler times—before Malakai revealed his secret. She let out a quiet sigh, stepping a bit closer to Maia. *Whatever happens*, she thought, *at least I have my best friend right here.*

And in that fleeting moment, with the sunshine warming her face, Aimee managed to set aside her turbulent worries. She resolved to face the pain in due course—maybe she would grant Malakai the chance to explain, or maybe not. But for now, she would cling to the small rays of comfort she still had, hoping that, in time, her faith in others—and perhaps in love—might not be entirely beyond repair.

CHAPTER FOURTEEN

Malakai surveyed his newly claimed office with a weary sort of satisfaction. Half-unpacked boxes lined the walls; his college diploma hung on a freshly painted patch of drywall, and a photo—one capturing a rare, relaxed moment with Aunt Rochelle years ago—perched on the corner of his desk. The place still smelled faintly of paint, intermingled with the comforting aroma of roasted coffee drifting from the diner's kitchen. *It's almost like home,* he told himself, though nerves still twisted in his stomach whenever he remembered why he was really here.

Aunt Rochelle—ever watchful and lively despite her self-declared "retirement"—maneuvered around a box stuffed with old folders. She paused at his framed diploma, then her gaze drifted to the photo on his desk. She picked it up, her features softening with affectionate nostalgia.

"I see you've started adding your own touch," she remarked with a playful gleam in her eye. "All it's missing is a color-coded schedule on the wall to scream 'Malakai.'" She laughed, the sound bouncing off the bare walls.

He mustered a tired grin, rubbing a persistent tension

behind his eyes. The days since revealing himself as the new owner had been a whirlwind of staff meetings, hurried phone calls, and last-minute policy changes. *At least Mr. Germaine is eager to cooperate,* he thought, trying to count his blessings. "The color-coded schedule is online," he said, rotating his laptop so she could see the bright swirl of color-coded blocks. "Right here. It shows when I'm in the office, on the floor, or out on break."

She nodded approvingly, her expression brimming with pride. "I picked the right guy for this, didn't I?" With a sigh, she settled into the worn leather seat opposite his desk. "So... have you had the chance to talk with Aimee yet? I see her soup is a runaway success."

At the mention of Aimee's name, his stomach tightened with guilt. *Of course she'd bring her up.* He shifted in his chair, forcing himself to focus on the bright blocks of his schedule. "No," he admitted quietly. "She's been off for a few days. But I plan on praising her recipe once she's back—maybe that'll ease some tension." The memory of Aimee's stricken face when she realized his true identity flared in his mind. "Honestly, part of me worries she won't want anything to do with me. But we have to talk for the diner's sake." *And for mine,* he added silently.

Rochelle pursed her lips, though her eyes held a hint of teasing. "You really think a bright, sweet girl like that is pining for you?" She shrugged in a matter-of-fact way. "She may well have moved on. But no harm in trying."

His stomach gave a disconcerting lurch. "You think so?" he asked, voice tight.

She raised an eyebrow. "Don't look so distraught. If you want to fix things, fix them. But don't drag your feet." With that, she rose gracefully from the chair and pulled open the office door. "Anyway, I'm up too early for a 'retired' woman. Don't forget to let me know how pretty Aimee reacts." She punctuated the remark with a playful wink before disappearing into the hall.

Malakai slumped back in his chair, staring at the closed door. The recollection of Aimee's hurt flashed across his mind for what felt like the hundredth time. *She was so angry—so betrayed.* He exhaled a shuddering breath. *And I caused that.*

He glanced at the photograph on his desk again—he and Rochelle laughing outside the diner one summer. "Pretty Aimee," he murmured, recalling Rochelle's phrase. But "pretty" didn't capture her warmth, her genuine passion for cooking, her readiness to serve others. She was so much more than an employee. *But does she even want to see me now?*

He forced himself to turn to his computer, his laptop's background a professional cityscape he'd once loved. Now it felt impersonal. With a few keystrokes, he worked through supplier emails, answered staff queries, and grimly typed out a new policy update. Eventually, a knock sounded on the door.

"Come in," he called, bracing for the next swirl of tasks.

Mr. Germaine stepped inside, offering a polite nod. "Aimee's clocked in," he informed, a note of curiosity coloring his voice. "I assume you wanted to know?"

Malakai's pulse leapt, and he had to fight to keep his expression neutral. "Yes," he said quietly. "Thank you. Could you ask her to come by the office for a quick chat? We've got... some business to address."

Mr. Germaine nodded, though his brow furrowed slightly—perhaps wondering if there was more to it. "Sure thing, boss," he replied, closing the door behind him.

Boss. The word struck Malakai differently than it used to. *I've always wanted to run a successful business, but not like this— hurting someone in the process.* He rolled his shoulders, trying to dispel the tension. *Calm down. This is about more than the diner now.*

Seconds ticked by like hours. At last, the gentle sound of

approaching footsteps reached his ears. The door cracked open, revealing Aimee in the familiar diner uniform—a crisp blouse and a neat blue skirt. Immediately, his heart throbbed with a mix of longing and regret. *She's here, but does she even want to be?*

She stepped in, posture reserved. Her gaze flicked over the half-unpacked boxes, then landed on him with cool detachment. "Sir, you wanted to see me?" she asked, voice clipped. That single word, *sir*, felt like a knife-edge partitioning them apart. Once upon a time, she'd said it teasingly. Now it sounded painfully formal.

Malakai swallowed, managing a nod. "Yes, Aimee. Please, have a seat." He gestured to the chair across his desk, noticing the way she perched stiffly on its edge. She looked ready to flee at any moment. A half-unpacked box to her left caught her gaze briefly before she folded her hands in her lap, leveling him with a measured stare.

He inhaled, carefully setting aside the swirl of emotions that threatened to swamp him. "I'm sure you've heard the good news." His voice sounded more uncertain than he liked. "Your soup has been a huge hit, so much so that we're struggling to keep up with demand. I'd like us to prepare more daily if you're up for it."

A flicker of pride danced across her features, but it was fleeting. "I'm… glad it's doing well," she replied, sounding as though she was forcing each word. She pressed her lips together, eyes sliding away from him.

He nodded. "It's well-deserved praise." He paused for a beat, then steeled himself. "But that's… not the main reason I asked you here."

She stiffened, glancing up warily. "Go on."

He leaned forward, resting his forearms on the desk. *Stay calm, be honest.* "Aimee, when I started coming into the diner, my plan was simple: watch how things ran without staff knowing I was the owner. I never expected to meet someone like you—

someone whose passion for cooking and friendly nature made me want to come back again and again." He searched her face for any sign of softening but saw only guarded apprehension.

Still, he pressed on. "I realize how badly I handled everything. The moment I started seeing how amazing you were, I should've confessed that I wasn't just some random customer. But I was afraid you'd treat me differently... or shut me out." His voice slipped, betraying the desperation he felt. "And the longer it went on, the harder it became to tell you. I'm sorry for the hurt I caused you."

Aimee's fingers tightened around the chair's arm. She said nothing, but her silence bore a sharp, wounded edge.

Malakai drew a breath, gaze locked on her. "I know you have no reason to believe me, but I—" He swallowed down a surge of anxiety. "I care about you. My admiration for your cooking was real, but it wasn't just about the diner. Talking to you was the highlight of every visit. Getting to know you was... is... one of the best things that's happened to me since returning to Sweetgum."

For a heartbeat, she held her breath, eyes flickering with some unspoken emotion. It might have been anger or sadness, or both. *Don't hold back now,* he urged himself.

"I fell for you, Aimee," he said, his voice trembling with sincerity. "I hate that I hurt you in the process. If I could rewind time and handle it differently, I would. But I can't." He inhaled sharply, bracing for the final blow. "I just want you to know the truth now: all of it. You deserve that much, at least."

He felt the silence loom, thick with tension and brimming with the hush of unsaid words. In the distant background, the diner's bustle persisted—plates clinking, a muffled laugh from the kitchen. Yet in this small office, the world had narrowed to the space between them.

At last, he forced out a final sentence. "I understand if you never want to talk to me again. But please... if there's any chance, I'd like a real conversation, with no more lies. I'm here, ready to answer anything."

Her eyes glimmered with conflicting emotions. She drew a hesitant breath, the tension in her shoulders so palpable he could almost feel it. The next heartbeat stretched into an eternity as he waited.

Is there hope here, or is this the end?

CHAPTER FIFTEEN

"*D*id you just say you fell for me?"

Aimee's question rang out before she could stop it. She stared at Malakai, heart pounding. "You… can't just say that," she managed, shaking her head in disbelief.

"I mean it," Malakai replied softly. "I know it probably sounds out of nowhere."

Her pulse throbbed in her ears. "It does. You never—" She paused, trying to steady her voice. "You never acted like that was what you wanted."

He exhaled, leaning forward over the desk. "I was undercover for business, yes. But then I kept coming back for you. I just—" He dragged a hand through his hair. "I never thought it'd turn into this."

She shot him a skeptical look. "All that time, you didn't give me one hint you had… deeper feelings. You were all business one minute, then distant the next."

Malakai swallowed. "I know," he admitted. "I messed up. I was juggling the diner stuff and—and realizing how I felt about you. It was confusing."

She folded her arms protectively, forcing her tone to stay calm. "Malakai, I can't just ignore how betrayed I felt. You popped up as a total stranger, only to reveal you're actually my new boss." She tried for a light laugh, but it wavered. "Did you really expect me to just trust you once you confessed everything?"

"No," he said quietly. "I expected you'd be angry. Hurt. That's why I'm asking for a chance now—to show you I wasn't lying about being drawn to you." He hesitated. "I get that you're cautious."

She pressed her lips together. "Of course I'm cautious. You lied about who you were for weeks. I might believe you had reasons, but that doesn't erase the damage."

Malakai nodded. "That's fair. But can you at least believe my feelings are real?" He held her gaze. "I've been trying to figure out how to tell you for days."

Her posture softened just a fraction. "I… maybe. I'm not sure." She let out a breath, glancing at the half-open office door. "You say you fell for me, but I spent a lot of time thinking you weren't interested at all."

His voice dropped lower. "I was interested from the start. Your drive in the kitchen, your warmth… everything. I just didn't know how to tell you without blowing my cover. Then it spiraled."

She brushed a stray curl from her face, struggling to form a response. The silence stretched, thick with unspoken questions. After a moment, she said, "Okay. I get your explanation. I'm still —adjusting to all of it."

He inched forward. "I'm sorry it's overwhelming. I can't change the past, but if you'll let me, I want to make it right."

Aimee looked at him evenly. "Make it right how?"

"Take you out," he offered, a faint smile touching his lips. "Let me prove I'm not just some 'undercover boss' who used you for intel. Show you I'm serious." He paused. "I understand if you say no. But I'm asking."

Aimee tilted her head. "A free dinner might help me think," she said with a faint, wavering grin.

He latched onto the hint of humor, nodding eagerly. "You pick the place. Anywhere. I'll be there."

She arched an eyebrow, crossing her arms again. "You sure you want to give me that much power?"

"I trust your judgment," he answered, smile growing. "And you know the best local spots better than I do."

She took a slow breath, glancing at the door again, suddenly aware of how visible they might be to passing staff. "Okay, fine," she said at last. "Dinner. I'll choose somewhere quiet. But don't think this fixes everything overnight."

Malakai's shoulders loosened with obvious relief. "I wouldn't dream of it. I just need a chance." He stood, coming around the desk. "And I'll do whatever it takes."

Aimee also rose, the tension in the room lifting an inch. She paused near the doorway, turning back to him. His expression—earnest and hopeful—made her chest flutter with conflicting emotions. "This is me taking a risk, Malakai," she warned softly. "Don't blow it."

He nodded gravely. "I won't. I promise."

She gave a small nod and stepped into the hall. Halfway down, she glanced over her shoulder, meeting his gaze one last time. Her heart beat unsteadily, but a shard of hope nudged her forward. "Tonight, then?"

"Tonight," Malakai confirmed, voice resolute.

She headed off, footsteps echoing against the diner's polished floors. At the corner, she slipped through the kitchen door, inhaling a breath laden with cooking spices. *One dinner—* that was all she'd agreed to. But the promise in Malakai's words hovered like an unspoken vow in her mind.

Yet the caution in her chest remained. *I'm giving him one chance,* she reminded herself, pushing away the memory of how easily he'd kept his secret. *One chance to show me it's not another lie.* And with that, she forced her focus on the busy swirl of the diner shift ahead, the half-formed swirl of anticipation and worry mingling beneath her measured composure.

CHAPTER SIXTEEN

Malakai checked his reflection in the rearview mirror for what felt like the thousandth time, fingers grazing the crisp edge of his fresh haircut. He could practically feel the tension sparking off his skin—an electric hum of nerves and anticipation that made his fingertips tremble. Outside, the soft glow of a streetlamp illuminated Aimee's two-story bungalow, casting delicate shadows across the yard. He'd been parked here for at least ten minutes, fiddling with every detail—straightening the collar of his shirt, rechecking his tie, adjusting his seat—anything to feel prepared for what he hoped would be a night that proved how serious he was about her.

He'd never been one to fuss over appearances. His childhood, spent partly in a boarding school environment, had taught him to grab whatever clothes were at hand and get on with the day. But tonight was different. Tonight, he wanted to transcend the label of "Malakai, the undercover nephew." He needed Aimee to see that he was more than a businessman who'd kept secrets—he was a man genuinely interested in **her**.

A lively pop song pulsed through the car speakers, its lyrics promising "the mother of all evenings." Malakai couldn't help but grin at the aptness of the words, though a twist of anxiety gripped his stomach. *Yes,* he told himself, *it really does need to be the mother of all evenings, because if I screw this up...*

His gaze swept back to the mirror, lingering on the tie's subtle sheen. **Was it too formal for a small-town date?** The color popped nicely against his jacket, though, and he decided it was a risk worth taking. *Stop overthinking,* he mentally scolded himself. *Focus on the reason you're here.*

That reason was enough to make his chest tighten. After confessing his true identity—and, more dauntingly, admitting that he'd fallen for her—Aimee had seemed torn: on one side, the hopeful glimmer in her eyes; on the other, the hurt that came from finding out he'd deceived her. He couldn't blame her for being guarded. But she'd still agreed to see him. Now, he was determined to make sure she knew just how genuine he was.

The radio's tempo shifted to an upbeat chorus, and Malakai released a long breath, rolling his shoulders. *Music always sets me straight,* he thought, letting the driving beat calm the flutter in his stomach. He wasn't a nervous kid heading to prom; he was a grown man, here to show the woman he cared for that she mattered beyond business or convenience.

He glanced out the window again, feeling his heart do a little flip at the sight of her snug, welcoming house. The porch light glowed gently, revealing a row of small potted plants flanking the front door. It looked warm, personal—very much like **her.** Through the living room window, a single lamp revealed a faint figure moving about. She was probably finishing her last-minute checks—keys, purse, phone.

Lowering his eyes to his phone, he reread her text (though he already knew it by heart):

Aimee: *Be out in 5! Don't go all business on me now... ;)*

He chuckled softly. She never sugarcoated what she was thinking. That unfiltered honesty was part of her charm. Even so, a sliver of doubt nagged at him. At the diner, she'd flashed him polite smiles, but he'd sensed the lingering caution in her gaze. Was she still holding him at arm's length?

Straightening the mirror one last time, he drummed his fingers on the gearshift. "All right, big guy," he whispered to himself, "it's go time." Fifteen minutes of waiting outside her place was probably enough to raise eyebrows among neighbors, anyway.

Suddenly, movement caught his eye—Aimee stepping out onto the porch, a navy cardigan draped over one arm. He felt his pulse spike. From the shape of her silhouette to the quick but graceful way she moved, everything about her made his heart slam with an exhilarating mix of nerves and anticipation. *She's actually coming.*

He popped out of the car, hurrying around to the passenger side as she approached. The night air was brisk, carrying the scent of damp leaves and the faint hush of a sleeping neighborhood.

"Hey!" she called, slowing when she saw him waiting by the door.

"Hey," he replied, letting his gaze roam over her appearance. "You look... amazing." And she did. The subtle overhead light brushed the outlines of her cheeks and the gentle curve of her lips, and as she drew near, a soft floral scent—like blossoms touched with berries—enveloped him. It felt like **her**.

A gentle flush swept her cheeks, but she smirked. "Thanks. You clean up pretty well yourself," she teased, noticing his tie with a once-over that made his stomach flutter.

He opened the car door with a small flourish, a gesture that sparked a laugh from her. As she settled into the seat, he inhaled that faint perfume, deepening the sense that he was stepping into something intimate. Then he closed the door carefully and made his way to his own side, forcing himself to breathe evenly.

"Sorry if I took too long," she said as he slid in behind the wheel, clicking her seatbelt. "I couldn't find my purse for a second."

Malakai's grin spread, though he prayed he didn't look too giddy. "Not a problem at all. I was just, uh..." He motioned to the radio, where the tune still bounced along. "Enjoying the music."

In truth, he'd been borderline panicking about everything—his tie, his hair, whether he smelled fresh enough—but she didn't need to know every detail of his freak-out. Right now, all that mattered was that she was here, in his passenger seat, wearing a deep red dress that flattered every curve, with a simple gold neckpiece glinting beneath the overhead dome light.

"Just as I guessed," she said, arching an eyebrow. "You're playing hype songs. Trying to get in the zone, are we?"

He chuckled, turning the volume down a notch. "Guilty as charged. I wanted to start the evening on the right note—literally."

She adjusted the skirt of her dress, crossing her legs with some difficulty in the car's limited space. "So," she said, that playful lilt in her voice. "Ready for me to guide you to some undisclosed location?"

He raised his brows in feigned worry. "Absolutely ready. But you're sure you won't give me a single clue? Even a cryptic one?"

Her eyes sparkled. "Consider it payback for your big secret. No hints. Now, you see that stop sign up ahead? Turn left there, and you'll be on track."

He let out a dramatic sigh, shifting into drive. "All right, all right," he said, easing the car away from the curb. The neighborhood glided by in a series of lit windows, well-tended lawns, and the occasional child's bike leaning on a fence. The sky overhead deepened from violet to dusky blue, the day's last light dissolving into the horizon.

A quick glance at her told him the excitement in her eyes matched his own. She might be cautious, but the sparkle was real. He flicked on his turn signal, thinking of how she'd walked into his life as just a friendly waitress, and how that had been flipped by his confession. Now, the small, swirling tension in his chest was overshadowed by relief. She'd come. She was giving him a chance.

She tugged her cardigan over her lap, rubbing the fabric's hem between two fingers. "It's so chilly," she murmured. "Probably should've worn something heavier."

"Want me to bump the heat up?" he asked, already reaching for the dial.

She nodded. "Just a little." As the heater kicked in, a soft current of warmth wafted between them, blending with the faint hum of the music and the quiet intimacy of the car.

He allowed a smile, letting the moment settle. "How was work?" he ventured, trying not to sound too stiff. "We saw each other briefly, but I, uh… wanted to save all the talking for tonight, I guess."

She looked at him from the corners of her eyes. "Honestly? It was fine. I kept thinking about this, so I might've been a little off my game." A corner of her mouth twitched. "Rochelle told me not to 'burn the kitchen down daydreaming.'"

Malakai choked out a laugh, imagining Rochelle's dramatic scolding. "And did you? Burn it down, I mean?"

Aimee rolled her eyes good-naturedly. "No, but I did almost forget to salt one of the dishes. That's a major sin in the cooking world, you know."

He grinned, relieved she was comfortable enough to share these small confessions. "In that case, I'll accept partial blame for your near-saltless fiasco."

Her shoulders shook with a quiet chuckle. The car slowed at another intersection, and she pointed. "Turn here. Then we'll be on the main road for a few minutes."

He nodded, flicking on the blinker. As they merged onto a slightly busier thoroughfare, the neon signs of local eateries glowed in the dusk. Groups of teens milled around the cinema, a couple strolled hand-in-hand, and a band of older men chatted outside a coffee shop. Malakai found it easy to envision strolling these streets with Aimee in a simpler time, maybe window-shopping or grabbing ice cream.

He caught himself *again* checking how her dress skimmed her figure. She was clearly more relaxed with him than she'd been earlier in the diner, her posture comfortable, her tone easy. It sent a jolt of pride through him. She wasn't freezing him out. She was letting him in, at least for tonight.

"I love me some good Italian," he said again, as if reaffirming his faith in her taste. "The diner's all about comfort food, so this is right up my alley."

Aimee smirked, fiddling with the radio dial to lower it further. "Wait until you see. This place does 'comfort' with a twist. I've tried a bunch of their pastas—absolute bliss."

He let the conversation meander into talk of favorite pasta dishes, gauging which ones might be too heavy for him. "You do realize," he said, half-laughing, "that if it's as good as you say, I might just camp out in front of the place every night."

She feigned exasperation. "And then I'd have to explain to Rochelle why her nephew is cheating on the diner's menu with fancy Italian. That's quite a scandal."

"Scandalous indeed," he teased, turning onto a quieter side street lined with older houses. "But you're the one leading me astray."

She let out a theatrical gasp. "Me? Leading you astray? I'd say I'm broadening your culinary horizons."

Their banter filled the space until she leaned forward, pointing at a softly lit sign shaped like an apple: **Fine Eats**. The cursive text below glowed gently. "We're here," she announced. "Welcome to my secret gem."

Malakai guided the car into a neat row of parking spots. Only a few vehicles dotted the lot, giving the impression of a cozy, intimate place. "I can't believe I've never noticed it," he murmured, cutting the engine. The radio died mid-chorus, leaving them in a hush that accentuated how close they were, how the overhead lamp in the car highlighted the warmth in her expression.

She slid her seatbelt off. "It's not huge—just enough to keep that homey vibe. Perfect for a quiet dinner."

He reached for the door handle. "Then let's see if the reality matches your hype, Ms. Aimee."

She waggled her eyebrows with mock superiority. "Oh, it will. I guarantee it."

He stepped out into the crisp evening, the air tinged with the faint smell of dried leaves and a passing whiff of fresh bread from somewhere unknown. Circling to her side, he caught her opening her door, but he offered a hand to help her out. She rolled her eyes lightly yet let him assist her, a playful smile tugging her lips as she slid out.

His heart quickened at the subtle brush of her fingers in his. The connection, even fleeting, reminded him why he was here: bridging the gap, proving he wasn't the man she'd feared, that he was genuinely interested in something beyond a short fling.

"Shall we?" she murmured, hooking her arm through his. The warmth of her body next to his made the corner of his mouth quirk up in a grin.

He nodded, leading her across the lot. Overhead, stars dotted the sky, a quiet painting of white freckles on midnight canvas. She matched his pace easily, the slight click of her heels on the asphalt a pleasant counterpoint to the hush of evening.

Pushing open the restaurant door, he let her step inside first. A wave of savory scents—garlic, oregano, melted cheese— engulfed them. His stomach grumbled in welcome. *Time for me to prove to her I can be more than just "Mr. Undercover."*

And as they stepped fully into the warm, inviting glow, he silently vowed to himself: *I won't let her down tonight, or any night after this.*

MALAKAI FOLLOWED the hostess to a booth along a wide, square-shaped window, its glass reflecting the restaurant's golden overhead lights. Beyond that reflection, he glimpsed the small parking lot—only a handful of cars left, an unexpected hush settling over the evening. Aimee slid in first, and he joined her across the table, the plush vinyl seat giving a soft creak under his weight. A gentle wave of heated air brushed his face, displacing the lingering chill from outside.

He let his gaze wander, taking in the polished auburn tiles that spread out in a precise grid, leading to neatly spaced tables. About five of those tables were still occupied, though all the diners seemed to be speaking softly, as if they shared in an unspoken agreement to preserve the cozy, intimate air. The light level was low but warm—enough to illuminate faces in a flattering glow. Together with the subdued murmurs of conversation, it felt like stepping into a small bubble that kept the rest of the world at bay.

A scent of basil and oregano teased Malakai's senses, underscored by a buttery richness that made his stomach clench in anticipation. *Definitely garlic too,* he thought, identifying the sweet tang of tomatoes simmering out of sight. The little touches—a few bright potted plants in the corners, the stone-textured décor reminiscent of rustic trattorias—added an authentic Italian vibe that felt both charming and welcoming.

"Wow," he breathed, leaning back slightly. "It's really nice in here." He kept his voice low, matching the mellow atmosphere.

Aimee brushed her fingertips across the smooth tabletop with an emphatic nod. "Right? It just feels… homey. Real Italian vibes." Her eyes lit up as she breathed in deeply through her nose. "Do you smell that?"

He raised his brow, amused at her excitement. "I smell plenty." Then, more purposefully, he inhaled. A swirl of something cheesy and savory greeted him. "Definitely cheese... maybe pizza? But there's a deeper aroma I can't quite name."

She smiled, clearly thrilled he was trying. "Cheese for sure—Parmesan, I'd guess. Plus butter, maybe a splash of wine." A quiet moment as she drew in a deeper breath. "Onions, too, so I'm betting on risotto. Thick, gooey risotto, the kind that practically melts on your tongue."

A laugh caught in his throat—part delight, part amazement. "All that from a single whiff?" He found himself leaning closer, almost hoping to catch the same intricacies she did. "I can tell it's delicious, but... picking out each ingredient like that is next-level."

Her cheeks warmed with modest pride. "I cook, remember? You basically enlisted me to make new soup recipes for the diner. After you spend enough time chopping and stirring, your nose starts to pick up on everything."

He couldn't hide his admiration. "We don't do Italian at the diner, but that's a seriously impressive sense of smell."

Aimee reached for the basket of breadsticks the waiter had discreetly placed between them. "It's more practice than talent," she insisted, cracking one open. A gentle puff of steam rushed out, carrying notes of butter and garlic straight to him. "I try new recipes at home constantly—some successful, some... not. But you learn to identify what's cooking in no time."

Malakai picked up a breadstick for himself, biting into its crisp exterior. The center was warm and tender, bursting with garlicky butter. He let out an appreciative hum. "That's incredible," he said around a mouthful, then swallowed. "You must've perfected a ton of dishes by now."

She gave a soft laugh that held a hint of pride. "I've lost

count, honestly. If you can name it, I've probably at least attempted it once."

He grinned broadly. "And yet, you still let me be your taste-tester? I'd be worried about scaring me off with experimental flops, but I guess your success rate is pretty high."

Shooting him a playful look, she broke off another bite of breadstick. "Don't forget you volunteered for that job. You practically begged to be my guinea pig when we were testing soups." Leaning in slightly, her tone turned conspiratorial. "And from what I hear, Rochelle's taste buds run in your blood. So you're more than qualified."

Malakai's chest warmed at that. "Rochelle's kin," he echoed her playful phrase. "Not sure I match her level of legendary palate."

Aimee's foot tapped lightly against the tiled floor, an unconscious sign of her energy. "Maybe not, but from what I've observed, you're no slouch in the flavor department." Then something glimmered in her eyes, a genuine curiosity. "What was it like being her 'secret relative' this whole time? You had to know so much about the diner—about us—but we had zero clues who you really were."

He set aside the half-eaten breadstick, the memory stirring a thoughtful smile. "She didn't exactly hide me," he explained. "Before the undercover idea, I'd visit in the summer, help her around the diner if needed, but mostly just laze around her house, devouring any new cake or stew she tested. She's always called herself the 'wisest woman in town,' and I guess she relished a little mystery."

Aimee's laugh was a melodic sound that made him feel at ease. "That's Rochelle for you. Loud, proud, and hilarious about it, too. She can boss a room like no one else."

He snickered, recalling countless times Rochelle had playfully bossed him around. "Oh, I know. One time, she caught me sneaking a second piece of triple chocolate cake. She gave me this huge lecture about sugar, *all while handing me the slice anyway.*"

They both laughed, and for a moment, the rest of the restaurant's subdued noise faded into the background. Malakai let her laugh wash over him, dissolving any leftover nerves.

Picking up the bread basket again, he noticed how quickly they'd polished off half the breadsticks. "We should probably save some space for the main course," he joked, though deep down, his hunger for the food was now rivaled by his hunger for *her* company.

Aimee took a small sip of water. "So, you spent those summers here, but I never spotted you. That's odd. Sweetgum's not big, and you're—kinda tall." She arched an eyebrow, as though sizing him up.

A flicker of vulnerability tensed his shoulders. "I wasn't social," he admitted softly, tapping at a stray crumb. "After losing my parents, I ended up in boarding school. Whenever I visited Rochelle, I mostly stayed inside. Reading, gaming… it was my safe zone. I probably just slipped under the radar whenever I did go out."

Her gaze softened. She reached across to give his arm a gentle squeeze. "I'm sorry," she said quietly. "That must've been lonely."

Warmth from her brief touch pulsed through him. "It was tough, but Rochelle was there. Always full of wisecracks and support." He paused, exhaling. "Anyway, that's why no one recognized me. I didn't get out much."

Aimee's hand fell away, but her empathy lingered in the air. "If I'd known you, I would've dragged you around town—ice cream stops, the old bleachers at the stadium… you name it."

He smiled, imagining a younger Aimee tugging a shy teen Malakai around. "I would've hated it for maybe ten seconds, then loved it the rest of the time."

They let a comfortable silence settle, Malakai taking a

moment to observe the restaurant around them. A couple across the way quietly stood, gathering coats and leaving a tip. Another table signaled for the check. Despite the mild commotion at the front, where a waiter chatted with the hostess, everything felt calm.

When Aimee broke the silence, her voice held a teasing edge. "So, aside from your big undercover strategy, were you ever a rebel as a kid? Rochelle didn't mention any troublemaker streak —maybe you were an angel?"

He grinned, recalling a half-forgotten memory. "In boarding school, I once feigned sickness for three days to skip classes. Got caught on day three, chilling at the campus food truck. Ended up cleaning the boys' locker room after a football game. Never repeated that stunt."

Her horrified laugh rang out quietly. "Yikes. Bet that was disgusting." She smirked, wagging a finger. "That's what you get for lying."

"Lesson learned," he said with mock solemnity. Then, noticing her mischievous look, he added, "What about you? No rebellious stories to share?"

She feigned innocence, lifting her chin. "I was a perfect student, obviously."

Malakai snorted, pointing a half-eaten breadstick at her as though accusing her of perjury. "Right. Sure you were. I can always ask Rochelle or the entire staff for the real story."

Aimee burst into a giggle, covering her face. "Fine, you got me. One time, in high school, I turned on the football field sprinklers to soak this snotty cheerleader who wouldn't stop harassing me. Never got caught, so in my mind it was the perfect crime."

He offered slow, mock applause. "Aimee, the stealth sprinkler vigilante. That's quite a mental image."

She giggled, her shoulders relaxing further. At some point during their banter, a waiter approached again, politely asking if they were ready to order. Aimee's eyes went wide at the reminder they'd barely looked at the menu.

They quickly settled on Fettuccine Alfredo, each admitting they found comfort in the dish's creamy richness. The waiter took the order, refilled their waters, and disappeared, leaving them alone with their conversation once more.

Malakai wiped a little ring of condensation from his glass with his napkin, then looked up. "So," he said, voice dropping in quiet sincerity, "did Rochelle ever talk about me during those summers? Or did she keep you all in the dark until she announced I was taking over?"

Aimee shook her head, an ironic smile tugging her lips. "Total dark. We had zero clue she even had a nephew, let alone that you'd become the new owner. People were floored at the announcement. You were, like… the biggest secret drop of the year."

He chuckled, imagining the staff's shock. "That's exactly the reaction we wanted. No special treatment for the boss if no one knows who he is." He paused, fiddling with his napkin. "I'll admit we might've gone overboard on the reveal. Rochelle does love a dramatic flourish."

"Tell me about it," Aimee said, sipping her water. A playful smirk took shape. "And now you're in cahoots with her. We have to keep an eye on you two conspirators."

He tilted his head, feigning innocence. "It's not all conspiracies—though maybe my aunt is cunning enough for that. But hey, now you and I share a circle with Rochelle. If that's not an honor, I don't know what is."

A gentle laugh escaped her. "She'll be missed at the diner. People practically cried when she declared she was retiring. I'm sure you felt the pressure stepping into that spotlight."

Malakai's chest tightened with the memory. "You have no idea. I respect what she's built. She's irreplaceable, and I just want to do right by her—and everyone else."

"You'll be fine," she replied gently. "Just... stay honest. No more surprises?" Her half-smile carried a hopeful note, as if she wanted to trust him fully but needed reassurance.

He dipped his head. "No more surprises," he promised. "It's all out in the open now."

They kept talking until their food arrived—two plates of creamy Fettuccine Alfredo, each garnished with a generous sprinkle of cheese and herbs. The aroma alone was enough to make Malakai's mouth water anew. He picked up his fork, swirling the pasta.

"Wow, it smells even better up close," he marveled.

Aimee was already savoring a bite, her eyes fluttering closed. "Mm," she murmured. "Creamy perfection."

They ate, letting conversation drift into small pockets of contented silence punctuated by remarks about the sauce's richness or whether the breadsticks were dangerously addictive. Malakai noted how the rest of the restaurant gradually emptied, though he hardly cared—**Aimee's company** was all he needed.

At some point, they found themselves in a spirited debate over classic film sequels, each defending their stance with passionate gestures. Malakai loved the sparkle in her eyes whenever she got animated—like a hidden fire. They bantered back and forth, occasionally pulling out random references. It felt effortless, natural, like they'd known each other longer than just a few weeks.

He was in the middle of mock-arguing his point when a polite voice interjected from the side. "Excuse me," the young waiter said, clutching his notepad, "but we'll be closing soon. You both have been here a while, and we just wanted to let you know..."

Malakai paused, glancing around, suddenly realizing the place was nearly empty. "Oh," he exclaimed softly. "We got totally carried away."

Aimee's eyes went wide in amused disbelief. "We're so sorry," she told the waiter, then exchanged a look with Malakai. "Guess we lost track of time. The food was amazing, by the way."

The waiter shrugged kindly. "No worries. We're just wrapping up. Take your time paying."

Malakai nodded, pocketing his phone. He rose from the booth, noticing how the staff had indeed started discreetly cleaning up. He gathered his wallet, and once again, Aimee offered to split the bill. He waved her off gently, insisting. "Let me," he said, pressing some bills into the waiter's hand. "You can treat me next time."

She rolled her eyes, but her smile said she was pleased. They made their way to the door, releasing small giggles like teenagers who'd lingered after curfew. The hush of the parking lot beyond was a stark contrast to the comfort of the restaurant, the sky overhead thick with stars, a faint breeze rustling through the last autumn leaves.

He cast her a sidelong glance, noticing the contented flush on her cheeks. "Wow," he remarked, a grin tugging at his lips. "Didn't expect we'd practically close the place."

Aimee shook her head, brows lifting. "Me neither. But it was fun," she admitted, pulling her navy cardigan around her as the night air brushed past. "I can't remember the last time I just ate, talked, and forgot about the clock."

His heart expanded at her confession. *I did something right tonight.* "I agree," he said. "I guess I should get you home, though, before we accidentally shut down every other place in town."

She smirked, tossing him a cheeky look. "Yes, Mr. Boss. Let's go."

MALAKAI EASED the car to a stop outside Aimee's house, cutting the engine just as the last chord of his favorite R&B track trailed off in the cabin. In the sudden hush, he became acutely aware of how much laughter and music had filled the drive over. Aimee's soft giggles still echoed in his mind, recalling the way she teased him about his "butchered but enthusiastic" singing.

Now, though, quiet descended. Neither of them moved. The cozy warmth they'd built up over the past hour—singing along to songs, bantering about old TV shows—seemed to hover in the confined space, a delicate bubble of closeness they both hesitated to break. Malakai turned his head slightly, and the faint glow of the streetlamp outside revealed the curve of Aimee's cheek and the reflective shine in her eyes.

Is she feeling the same? he wondered, pulse jittering. *Like everything's about to shift once we leave this car?*

In that short silence, she shifted her hand on her lap, drawing his attention. There was a subtle tension to the moment, like they both recognized the closeness they'd found—and how delicate it was. At last, she turned toward him, and he swiveled at the same time. Their eyes locked, a flicker of mutual awareness sparking in the dim light. Something deeper seemed to settle between them—something unspoken yet undeniably present. "I'll walk you to the door," he offered, his voice gentler than intended. "Would you like that?"

She gave a quick, emphatic nod, almost as if she'd been hoping he'd offer. "Yes," she answered, her voice hushed. A faint tension thrummed under the quiet, sending a ripple of aware-ness along Malakai's spine.

They climbed out into the autumn air, which felt cooler after the enclosed heat of the car. Leaves rustled faintly across the pavement, and the porch light cast a welcoming glow over the short walkway to her door. Malakai led the way up the steps, each footstep sounding loud in the evening stillness. Malakai could almost feel the quiet hum of energy between them, making his fingertips tingle in anticipation.

She stopped near her front door, keys in one hand, her bag in the other. Her gaze lifted, meeting his with a softness that made his chest tighten. He noticed the slight tension in her posture, as though she wasn't quite sure how to end the night but wasn't ready for it to be over.

"I had fun tonight," he said, allowing a small, genuine smile to edge onto his face. "I didn't realize how much I needed an evening like this."

Her lips curved, echoing his sentiment. "Me too," she murmured, fiddling lightly with her bag's strap. "You know… after your whole 'big reveal'—" she let out a soft, rueful laugh "—I kept replaying all our previous conversations, thinking, 'How is this guy possibly Rochelle's nephew?'"

Malakai let a grin slip across his face, though a breeze grazed his cheek, reminding him how close she stood. "So what did you conclude?" he teased, a thread of caution in his words. "That I'm a total disappointment next to the legendary Rochelle?" In truth, he was half-worried she might say yes.

A glimmer of amusement lit her expression. She reached out, tapping his shoulder in a playful scold. "Not at all," she said firmly. "Actually, I see *her* in you—the vibrant side, that spark of passion. At first, you seemed so laid-back, but the more we've talked, the more I catch glimpses of that same energy Rochelle has."

An unexpected thrill coursed through him. "Maybe I'm on the nutty side, like my aunt," he joked, though there was tenderness in his tone. Being compared to Rochelle in a positive way felt oddly comforting. But overshadowing it all was the realization that Aimee was, once again, stepping closer, stepping into his space.

She pressed a forefinger to her lips in mock scolding. "Hey now, I said *spirited*, not nutty," she corrected, a quiet laugh escaping. "But I did really enjoy tonight. Talking… laughing… no pressure."

Malakai slid his hands from his pockets, letting them hang loosely by his sides. Her nearness drew every fiber of his attention, the subtle perfume she wore lingering on the night air. "So," he ventured, "that means we might do this again sometime? Soon?" He tried for a light, teasing pout, hoping she'd indulge him.

She scrunched her nose as though seriously considering. "Oh God, no," she deadpanned. His heart jumped, but then she broke into a grin. "I'm kidding. Yes, I'd love to."

He let out an audible sigh of relief, and a quiet laugh bubbled between them. The mild tension turned sweet, making him extra aware of the short distance separating their bodies. "Don't scare me like that," he murmured, noticing the shape of her lips and forcing himself to keep his gaze on her eyes. "Next time, maybe you can show me how to use all those fancy spices you keep talking about. Or, I don't know, teach me how to chop onions without crying?"

She rolled her eyes, amusement dancing at the corners of her lips. "I'll do my best. But some onions make you weep no matter how tough you are. And you're tough, right?"

He gave a playful shrug. "Tough enough to handle your cooking lessons," he quipped, though his voice wavered with something deeper. Because in that moment, the distance between them felt too small to ignore—and too compelling to break away from.

A hush lingered, overshadowing the last of their banter. She rocked on her heels, an unconscious gesture that only heightened the tension. The light from the porch lamp caught on her features, accentuating the anticipation in her eyes. Malakai felt it coursing through his own body—a gentle, undeniable pull to close that final gap.

"We'll talk," he managed to say, voice dropping in pitch. Acting on impulse, he took a half-step closer, raising one hand from his side. The rest of the world receded: no distant bark of a dog, no subtle hum of passing cars. All that existed was the flicker of her breath, the slight parting of her lips, and the warmth emanating from her presence.

He tilted his head, leaning in so their faces were mere inches apart. Instead of aiming for her lips, he pressed a soft, lingering kiss to her cheek. The tender contact flooded his senses—her skin carrying that sweet, floral hint, the faintest quiver of her breath as she took in the moment. He lingered just a beat longer than he'd planned, and in that heartbeat, felt her body give the smallest lean toward him, as though she might accept more if he dared.

But he eased back, his heart thundering in his chest. Clearing his throat, he retreated a step, aware that any further might be pushing too far, too soon. "Goodnight," he said, voice huskier than normal. He couldn't quite look her in the eye as he spoke, too overwhelmed by the rush of emotions pounding in his veins.

She blinked, her cheeks glowing under the porch lamp. A soft murmur of breath left her, and she nodded faintly. "G-goodnight," she answered, the faint trace of surprise on her face. But Malakai also saw something that resembled hope—or maybe even invitation—behind that stunned expression.

He managed a short, curt nod and turned toward his car, forcing himself not to linger. Part of him ached to see her full reaction, to maybe chance one more step. But caution told him not to rush. He was determined not to break the fragile trust blossoming between them.

Sliding into the driver's seat, he started the engine, every nerve still humming from that soft contact of his lips on her skin. He gripped the steering wheel, stealing a look through the windshield. Sure enough, Aimee still stood on her porch, keys in hand, gazing after him with what looked like a gentle daze. That fleeting second of eye contact across the yard pulsed with more warmth than he ever thought a simple cheek kiss could conjure.

Starting the engine, he lifted his fingers in a small wave, and she returned it, her lips curving in a near-tremulous smile. Even as he backed onto the quiet street, he caught one last glimpse of her stepping inside, a final wave in the golden light. His chest felt buoyant, his grin unstoppable.

He navigated the empty roads back toward his own apartment, the adrenaline of that sweet, lingering moment pumping through his veins. Each streetlamp's glow reminded him of her porch light, the place where he'd worked up the nerve to lean in just a little. As the car stereo resumed another pop ballad, he found himself quietly humming along, unselfconscious of any wrong notes.

So much for feeling uncertain. Tonight had ended in a way he scarcely dared hope for—a soft, intimate promise that tomorrow could hold even more. The memory of her cheek's warmth still tingled on his lips, and the knowledge that she'd accepted his next invitation fueled a sense of excitement he couldn't contain.

Yes, there was caution. Yes, there were still issues to navigate —but there was also this undeniable spark that flared higher each time they dared step closer. Malakai drove on, a small, unstoppable smile illuminating his face in the darkness. He let the thought of that final wave, that faint pink flush on her cheeks, carry him home in a haze of contentment.

CHAPTER SEVENTEEN

Aimee hadn't planned on their second date happening only a few days after the first, nor had she expected the third to follow hot on its heels. Yet every time Malakai texted or called with an invitation—ranging from coffee runs to exploring local fall markets—she found herself eagerly saying yes. By the time October rolled in, they'd gone from hesitant flirtation to a slow-blooming partnership that made her heart race in the sweetest way.

The first date had felt like dipping a toe into unknown waters, both of them careful not to scare the other off. But by the second, Aimee realized she was already looking forward to the moments between the laughter—those quiet pockets where Malakai would lean in, his voice low and intimate, asking about her day. He seemed genuinely interested in who she was, not just what she did. And after the third date, that sense of closeness only grew deeper. He learned her favorite coffee order, how to coax her out of her shell if she was feeling tense, and she discovered the gentleness beneath his ready grin.

It was barely two weeks of seeing each other consistently when he brushed a soft kiss over her cheek and murmured,

"We're good together, aren't we?" She'd felt breathless, almost giddy, when she answered, "I think so," and pressed a kiss to his temple in return. A simple conversation—yet it left them with the mutual understanding they were officially a couple.

By the time Halloween came around, it felt completely natural to plan a silly, matching costume. Aimee found herself grinning every time she thought about it: them, together, going public in that unspoken way that couples do when they dress in theme. And so, on the crisp October evening of the town's indoor pumpkin festival, she had never felt prouder of a Halloween costume in her entire life.

Over the years, she used to quietly judge couples who wore coordinated getups, finding it a bit too cutesy or contrived. But that was before she became half of a pair—this pair, to be exact. Ever since she and Malakai made their relationship official a couple of weeks ago, she realized how fun it could be to share little moments of silliness like matching outfits.

Tonight, they'd chosen to dress as a chef duo—her as the head chef, him as her, allegedly, humble apprentice. The small, tongue-in-cheek detail that delighted her most was the name tag pinned to his coat reading, She's My Boss. It matched her own, which declared, I'm In Charge. They'd enjoyed a flurry of laughs putting it all together, and she still felt a ripple of amusement whenever she caught sight of their matching white jackets in a mirror.

Malakai walked beside her through the busy pumpkin festival, his phone out, snapping photo after photo. He was so easily intrigued by everything, she mused with an affectionate grin—one more reason I like him. The festival took place indoors this year, the town's old gym-turned-event space transformed by rows of vibrant pumpkin displays. A large orange banner overhead announced "Harvest Celebration," and the chatter of families and couples filled the air in an almost musical hum.

They stopped at one farmer's table that sported an enormous, bright-orange gourd, carved with swirling designs. Malakai let out a low whistle, leaning in to get a better angle for a picture.

"Look at that," he breathed, touching Aimee's arm gently so she could share the moment. "It's so intricate—like an art piece instead of just a pumpkin."

Aimee's heart gave a small flutter at his soft touch. Over the past two weeks, she'd grown delightfully accustomed to the way he'd rest a hand on her back or curl an arm around her waist in casual affection. She murmured back, "It is beautiful." She tilted her head to inspect the swirls. "Makes me think of fancy latte art or something."

The farmer stood proudly behind his display, chest puffed. He tipped his wide-brimmed hat in their direction. "Took me a whole day to carve it," he said. "Hope y'all enjoy."

Malakai snapped a few more pictures, then shifted closer to Aimee. His free hand gently squeezed her waist, and she felt the warmth of his palm through her chef's coat. The small gesture made her pulse speed up—more than she would've admitted on their first date, but now it simply thrilled her.

"I love that you're so willing to drag me around these local events," he teased in a low tone.

"Hey, you're the one taking pictures of every single pumpkin," she shot back, nudging his side playfully. "Not that I mind. I like seeing you get so hyped."

He brushed a light kiss to her temple—brief, almost as if checking to see if it was okay. She shot him a quick, conspiratorial smile that said it definitely was. Ever since they'd become a couple, these little shows of affection had become both exhilarating and comforting in equal measure.

They moved along to the next stand, where an older gentleman was showing off a bright, painted pumpkin with a goofy, toothy grin. Aimee leaned over the table, genuinely impressed by the detail in the painted features.

"Adorable," she told the man.

He dipped his head in thanks, then gave their costumes an approving once-over. "Y'all headed for a kitchen after this?" he asked, voice warm with curiosity. "Those uniforms look mighty fine for Halloween."

Aimee couldn't help a laugh. "Thank you. It's a little inside joke we have," she said, glancing at Malakai. "He's my apprentice, apparently."

Malakai clasped a hand to his chest in mock sincerity. "I'm just following orders, sir," he joked. "But she's been showing me I'm not half bad at whipping up a meal when I try."

The man chortled good-naturedly and waved them on. Aimee couldn't wipe the smile off her face as they meandered among the displays, greeting a few neighbors she recognized from the diner. *It's been a while since I've felt this light,* she thought. *Dating Malakai... it feels surprisingly comfortable.*

From overhead speakers, a sudden announcement rang out, "Attention, folks! Our Harvest Parade on Main Street will begin in ten minutes! Please head outside to enjoy the floats and music. Thank you!"

A wave of excitement rippled through the crowd, and families began drifting toward the exit. Malakai linked his fingers with hers.

"Want to check it out?" he asked, giving her a gentle tug that sent warm tingles up her arm.

Aimee nodded, the corners of her mouth quirking up. "I wouldn't mind seeing what they've come up with this year. Last year was a blast, so I'm sure they're going big again."

With an easy laugh, they wove their way through the throng of costumed visitors, sometimes pausing so Malakai could snap a photo of a cleverly carved pumpkin. Each time he paused, he rested a possessive hand against the small of her back, making her hyperaware of the soft friction through her chef's coat. Every small touch he offered her felt like a promise—a wordless way of saying, *I'm here, and I'm yours.*

She pressed in closer to him as they headed outside, stepping into the crisp evening air. The sky glimmered with faint stars, a backdrop for the glowing streetlamps that lit up Main Street. A half-dozen floats lined up a short distance away, each decorated with fall motifs: bales of hay, fake leaves in shades of burnt orange, and cartoonish pumpkins. Music drifted from a loud-speaker, the melody cheerful and old-timey, fitting the small-town vibe perfectly.

"This is definitely bigger than last year," Aimee observed, spotting elaborate homemade costumes among the crowd. She saw fairies with glittery wings, a wizard family, even someone dressed as a giant ear of corn. Kids squealed and ran about, while older folks set up folding chairs along the curb. She made sure to stay close to Malakai, not wanting to get separated in the slowly growing throng.

He lifted their joined hands briefly, giving her knuckles a soft brush with his thumb. "I love how everyone's so into it," he said, voice brimming with genuine admiration. "In the city, events get massive, but you lose that personal touch. Here, it's like we're all part of one extended family."

She shot him a tender smile, feeling that familiar flicker in her stomach that signaled just how much she was enjoying his presence. "Exactly," she agreed. "It's one reason I can't imagine leaving Sweetgum. I love the closeness—like if I vanish for a week, someone's definitely going to pop by to check on me."

Malakai chuckled, sliding an arm around her waist now. She felt the warmth of his side pressing gently against hers as they strolled in search of a good vantage point. "I might not be a Sweetgum native," he said, "but I think I'm catching the spirit just fine."

A wave of horns and clapping signaled the parade's official start. One by one, the floats began to roll down the street, each with a theme: Scarecrows for the first, a haunted barn motif for the second, all culminating in a grand "Harvest Bounty" float stacked high with pumpkins and cornstalks. The air buzzed with excitement; passersby cheered, kids waved from the sidewalks, and costumed volunteers on the floats tossed small candies into the crowd.

Aimee clapped along, letting out small exclamations every time a float's music changed or a new character popped up. Malakai, for his part, occasionally murmured commentary in her ear—little remarks about how elaborate some decorations were. She felt each breath he took as his chest brushed her shoulder, his quiet observations sending small thrills through her. *I could get used to this closeness,* she admitted to herself, leaning slightly against him.

They watched for another ten minutes, and Aimee stole a glance at her phone's screen. Time was slipping away faster than she realized, and she had another plan for the night: Maia's Halloween party. They'd promised to swing by with the treats Aimee had made, and it was creeping close to the start time. *We can't stand here too long, or I'll miss seeing Maia's reaction to our costumes—and the homemade goodies,* she thought.

She tugged on Malakai's sleeve gently, turning so he could hear her over the raucous brass band playing on the last float. "It's probably time we head out. We don't want to miss Maia's party, right?"

He checked his own watch, blinking in mild surprise. "Wow, you're right—look at the time." His arm slipped from her waist, and he let their fingers intertwine instead. "Let's go."

They threaded back through the crowd, weaving around a group of teenagers dancing to the band's final tune. Gradually, the noise faded as they neared the lot where Malakai had parked. Each step felt like an echo of the warm light they left behind, but Aimee's excitement remained high—there was more evening to savor.

He opened the passenger door for her with a small flourish, and she rewarded him with a gracious little dip of her head in mock formality. Climbing into the seat, she smoothed her makeshift chef's apron, careful not to wrinkle it. When Malakai slid in beside her and started the car, she turned with an appreciative grin.

"Thank you, good sir," she teased.

He returned a playful bow, then reversed out of the spot. "Anything for the head chef," he teased back, reaching once again to brush his knuckles against her knee, a light, affectionate touch that had her heart fluttering. She liked how natural it felt—these small, electric moments of contact.

As he drove through the quieter side streets, the low hum of the engine providing a soothing backdrop, Aimee leaned her head back against the headrest. She couldn't keep a small smile from lingering on her lips. They'd spent weeks building this sense of closeness, a gentle push-and-pull of flirting and confiding in each other. Now, each shared joke or easy silence felt like proof that they were weaving something real.

"Ready for your next shift, Ms. Chef?" Malakai asked, one brow arched as they turned onto a familiar road. "I hear Maia's hosting a grand soiree, complete with costumes and questionable party games."

Aimee rolled her eyes good-naturedly. "Maia's parties are always a riot. I can't wait." She flicked a glance at the back seat where boxes of her treats were carefully arranged. "I hope the goodies didn't shift around too much with all that weaving through traffic."

Malakai cast her a quick reassuring smile. "They're fine, I promise. I made sure to drive like I'm transporting priceless cargo." He reached out, lacing their fingers together again. "But if you're worried, I'll keep the speed down," he joked, tone playful.

She laughed softly, a thrill dancing in her chest at the hand-holding—a simple gesture, but that gentle friction between their palms wasn't something she could ignore. "Thank you," she whispered, turning her face to the window as the dim shapes of houses slid past.

Yet she felt the weight of his gaze on her profile—warm, interested, maybe even a little hungry. She let her eyes close for a second, absorbing the quiet moment. *Yes,* she thought, *this is all I wanted for so long—a real connection.*

The car picked up a little speed once they hit an open stretch, and Aimee's pulse danced faster in response. She realized, with a small rush of gratitude, that she was every bit as excited to see Maia's party as she was to keep enjoying Malakai's company for the rest of the evening. *He's showing me that maybe sweet romance is possible, after all,* she mused, leaning toward him just enough so her shoulder brushed his. He squeezed her hand once more, his answering touch like a promise that the night was far from over.

And as the glow of streetlights played across the hood, Aimee couldn't stop the little grin tugging her lips. The Harvest Parade might be ending, but her evening with Malakai had only begun—and that thought sent a pleasant, shivery anticipation down her spine.

CHAPTER EIGHTEEN

Spooky tunes, grinning jack-o'-lanterns, and a home packed with costumed guests—Maia's Halloween party spilled from the front door onto the lawn, the pulsating music audible from the sidewalk. Aimee and Malakai navigated the press of bodies in the hallway, the flickering orange and green lights transforming the space into a makeshift club. On her tray, she balanced another batch of freshly restocked snacks. No matter how often she refilled them, people kept gobbling everything up, she thought with pride.

"And you made all of this?" The question came from Brandi Astore, a friendly face Aimee had seen around town. They both hovered in the lit-up kitchen, which served as party headquarters for food and drinks, while every other room flashed with colored lights. Brandi's husband, Chris, leaned against the counter behind her, sipping from a red plastic cup containing a Halloween punch.

Aimee smiled as Malakai poured punch into her own cup. She let her gaze wander to the living room, where costumed partygoers swayed in time to a spooky remix. She and Malakai had started an impromptu game of counting how many women dressed as bunnies they could spot—they were already on four. Her grin widened. We're so silly together sometimes, she mused happily. "Well, I can't claim the punch," she said, giving the red liquid a stir, "but I made the sandwiches, caramel apples, kabobs, cookies, and spicy fried chicken."

"Wow," Brandi said, sounding impressed above the thump of the music. "I've probably eaten six kabobs, and Chris can't get enough of the sandwiches."

Chris raised his cup in a toast, mouth curving into a grin. They were dressed as matching prisoners, black-and-white stripes crossing their torsos. "She's not lying," he admitted with a chuckle. "I'm worried the snacks'll run out soon if I don't pace myself."

"That's why she's the boss," Malakai declared. Pride suffused his tone as he tapped a hand against Aimee's waist, inching a bit closer. "She makes everything perfect—food, and, well… everything else." He swayed in time to the heavy beat. "And she's also the genius behind that pumpkin soup at the diner, if you haven't tried it yet. Huge hit."

Aimee felt her cheeks warming and lightly covered Malakai's mouth with her palm to hush his enthusiastic rambling. Brandi and Chris looked amused, exchanging a knowing look.

"Someone's excited," Aimee teased, pressing her other hand to Malakai's forearm. "He's never been to a house party before—can you tell?"

He peeled her hand away gently but grinned. "Not *never*," he corrected, sliding a warm palm to rest at the small of her back.

Brandi's eyes lit as though a puzzle piece had clicked. "Oh, so that's what your costumes mean—she's the head chef, you're the sous chef. It's a cute way of telling the world who's in charge." She winked at Aimee with genuine delight.

Chris chuckled, pointing to his prisoner stripes. "Yeah, we like to think ours does the same—though in our case, we're both troublemakers." He shot Brandi a playful look, then softened. "Kidding. She's amazing with kids. The patience she has? I've never seen anything like it."

Aimee's heart melted a bit; it reminded her that some couples in this town really had that special spark. "That's awesome," she said. "Herding kids all day sounds downright impossible to me. Good on you both."

"Seriously," Malakai added. He offered Brandi a light fist bump. "We salute you. Hey, I think the song changed—listen!" He perked up as the beat shifted to a more energetic track. A roar of excitement echoed from the living room, guests flooding there to dance.

Aimee caught Malakai's hand, felt the heat of his fingers twining with hers. "C'mon," she urged, setting down her cup. "I love this song!"

He grinned down at her, and she noticed the flash of excitement in his eyes as they followed the crowd onto the makeshift dance floor. The living room lights flickered orange and green, turning them into silhouettes among other dancing bodies. Aimee found herself pulled into Malakai's arms, the playful rhythms guiding them as they bobbed and swayed, matching each other's energy.

She gave herself over to the pulse of the music, feeling the brush of Malakai's costume against hers each time they pivoted. When the song morphed into another lively tune, he dipped her theatrically, earning cheers from a few onlookers. *He's not half-bad,* she thought, giggling as he spun her upright again.

Eventually, a slower piece trickled through the speakers, shifting the mood. Malakai's hold on her became more intimate, his hand sliding around her waist, drawing her nearer. She felt the warmth of his body pressed close, her heart thumping with a delicious tension that hadn't been there before.

"I think the kabobs ran out," he murmured near her ear, his breath teasing her skin. His voice held a mischievous undertone, but the closeness—his chest against hers—made her pulse skip.

She lifted her face to catch his gaze. "I'm not surprised. People *did* devour them." Her voice came out a bit huskier than intended. She attempted to gather herself by looking around the room. The neon lights danced across smiling faces, while outside, more guests lounged on the porch. "I'm glad they're enjoying everything." Maia had done a spectacular job with decorations, though Aimee realized she hadn't seen her friend in a while—likely off greeting everyone in her own costume glory.

Malakai nodded, leaning his forehead briefly against hers as they swayed. "Yeah, Maia really outdid herself," he said, then placed a light, lingering kiss on Aimee's forehead. The gesture sent a gentle flutter through her chest—sweet but leaving her wanting more.

"And so did you," he added, quiet pride etched in his tone. "I'm thinking we could use some of these snacks at the diner, especially if people love them this much. Maybe have them as an appetizer menu—"

Aimee pressed her palm to his chest, feeling the steady thump of his heartbeat under her touch. She gave a playful roll of her eyes. "Malakai," she chided gently. "Don't tell me the diner is all you think about—especially at a Halloween party."

He hesitated a fraction of a second, maybe realizing how single-minded he sounded. "I just... think we could up our game. The menu—"

She silenced him by softly pressing a finger to his lips, an affectionate smile curving her mouth. "Shh," she said. "We can talk about the diner on Monday. Tonight, I want time with my *boyfriend,* not my boss."

He exhaled slowly, laughter tinged with relief. "Got it," he teased, his lips curling. Then, acting on impulse, he replaced her fingertip with a gentle kiss—a fleeting press of his mouth to hers.

It wasn't overly bold, just a brief brush of lips that sent a sudden spark from her head to her toes. Aimee felt her breath catch, every nerve startling awake as the music thrummed around them. The taste of his lips, just for that heartbeat, held the promise of more, if they let it happen. She parted slightly, meeting his gaze, her heart fluttering like she'd just sprinted a mile.

Her eyes flicked to his mouth, and she almost forgot there was a party swirling around them. "M-Malakai," she murmured, a small smile tugging at her lips, cheeks glowing from the inside out.

His own eyes glinted with a mixture of fondness and barely contained desire. "Sorry," he whispered, not looking sorry at all. "Is that allowed at this party?"

Aimee could only manage a bemused look. "I think so." Her arms slid up to loop around his neck, lingering in that charged closeness. She let out a quick laugh to steady the intensity.

He grinned mischievously, moving his hands around her waist once more. "I can always steal you away after the party and kiss you in private," he joked, voice low, sending another wave of warmth rushing through her.

"Deal," she managed, leaning against him as the slow track ended. The crowd erupted into cheers, and a new surge of energy pulsed around them. But Aimee still felt the hum of that kiss vibrating in her chest.

Malakai pressed his forehead to hers briefly, as if savoring the last note. "So, no more diner talk," he promised in a whisper. "For the rest of tonight, I'm at your disposal, Head Chef."

She snorted softly but felt a sweet tingle lingering on her lips. "I'll hold you to it," she teased, catching his gaze one last time before tugging him away from the dance floor. They returned to the flow of the party, hand in hand, hearts pounding with the promise that the best moments of the evening—and of their story—were still unfolding.

AIMEE COULD STILL FEEL the pulse of the music reverberating through her veins as Malakai pulled his car into her driveway. Even with the engine off, her heart thumped in her chest like it was keeping time to the party beat still thrumming in her memory. The porch light illuminated her little bungalow, casting long shadows across the lawn. Somewhere in the distance, a breeze rustled through leaves, the only sign that it was nearing midnight.

They sat in contented silence for a moment. A sense of breathless exhilaration lingered in the car, a hush wrapping around them after hours of laughter and dancing. Every small movement Malakai made—the shift of his hand on the steering wheel, the gentle clench of his jaw—caught her attention. *We can't just sit here all night,* she thought with a faint smile.

He glanced at her, their eyes locking in the muted glow of the dashboard lights. "Ready?"

She swallowed hard, the air in the car suddenly thick with promise. "Yeah," she murmured.

Malakai exited the car to open her door. Aimee climbed out, and the short walk from the passenger seat to her front porch felt like a slow-motion journey. Every step magnified the pull between them, the tension that had been building since their dance. Her costume's chef coat still smelled faintly of spices and the warmth of the party. His "apprentice" jacket brushed her side as they reached her front door.

Aimee fumbled with her keys, keenly aware of Malakai standing behind her, close enough that she felt the heat radiating off his body. The key slid into the lock, but before she could turn it, a gentle pressure at her shoulder made her pause.

She turned, looking up into his eyes—close enough to catch the woodsy scent of his cologne and the heightened emotion in his gaze.

He spoke softly, like a confession. "You have no idea how hard it was not to kiss you every second back there."

Aimee's pulse jumped at the electricity in his voice. She drew in a breath, unguarded words tumbling out: "I wouldn't have minded." She tried for a casual smile, but the longing was far beyond casual.

Malakai's gaze flicked to her mouth, and in one fluid motion, he leaned down, capturing her lips in a slow, searing kiss. The door keys jingled in her hand as she abandoned the lock, pressing a palm against his chest to steady herself. She felt the thud of his heartbeat through the thin fabric, matching the quick rhythm of her own.

His lips were firm yet coaxing, swirling warmth low in her belly. She tasted the remnants of sweet punch, felt the eager slide of his hand down her waist. Different from the lighter kisses they'd shared—this was charged with all the tension simmering throughout the night. She leaned up on her toes, wanting to drown in the moment.

When they finally broke apart, she clutched his coat for balance, breath uneven. Her lips tingled, and she forced herself to speak. "Malakai," she whispered, a hint of urgency in her tone. "Do you… want to come in for a bit?"

He swallowed, gaze locked on her. A faint rasp caught in his voice. "If you'll have me."

She exhaled a laugh that was half relief, half anticipation. Twisting the key, she managed to open the door. The house was quiet, darkness swallowing them. Without flipping the hallway switch, she guided him inside. The hush felt intimate, heightening her every sense. She let the door click shut behind them.

They navigated the shadows to the small lamp in her living room. With a soft click, a warm glow spilled over her comfy sofa and scattered pillows. She slipped off her shoes, and Malakai followed suit, occasionally letting his gaze linger on her figure in a way that made her heart stutter.

"Was that your first real house party?" she teased lightly, trying to find a stable note amid the heady tension.

He half-smiled. "Guess you could say that." Then he drew closer, brushing his fingertips along her bare forearm. A subtle, magnetic pull guided them to the sofa. "I'm not complaining, though—especially if it ends like this."

Aimee's heart pounded. She sank onto the cushions, and he settled beside her, not quite touching, but near enough that the air felt electric between them. Clearing her throat, she clutched a throw pillow to her chest, her eyes drifting to the strong lines of his jaw, the lamplight playing across his features.

"I... had a really amazing time," she began quietly. "You're so different when you're relaxed. Not the boss, or Rochelle's nephew, or the 'undercover guy.' Just… Malakai."

He pivoted toward her, sliding a hand over her knee, the contact sparking a tingling heat. "I want you to know me *like this*," he admitted, voice dipping low. "Not just the me at the diner, or the me playing a role. The real me, flaws and all."

She swallowed hard, emotion warming her chest. "I'm trying," she managed, a fragile grin curling her lips. "Though it's hard to keep my head when you do things like…" She flicked her gaze to his hand on her leg. "…that."

Malakai's laugh rumbled softly. He lifted his palm, tracing upward until it rested at her waist. "Then I'll keep it up," he murmured, leaning in until their foreheads nearly touched.

Aimee's breath caught, her pulse skittering. She could sense him inching closer, the woodsy cologne wrapping around her like a promise. All the tension from the party, the electric friction of their dance, coiled tight now, waiting to snap.

He kissed her once, gently, but it quickly deepened. She met his passion, a low hum escaping her throat as her fingertips found the collar of his uniform and tugged him nearer. Their mouths moved together in a slow, simmering dance that soon burned with more urgency, each breath melding into the next.

Her mind spun with desire and a flurry of questions—*Could this be too fast?*—but the press of his mouth felt devastatingly right, banishing any doubts. He broke the kiss just enough to whisper her name, eyes searching hers. She saw the same need, the same surrender reflected back at her.

They didn't need further words. Aimee stood, guiding him by the hand down the short hallway toward her bedroom. The lamplight faded with each step, but their ragged breathing filled the hush.

At the threshold, Malakai lifted a hand to gently cup her cheek. The tenderness in his expression made something in her chest twist. In answer, she pulled him into another kiss, letting it speak for her, letting it express every bit of trust and hope she couldn't yet voice. The tension that had simmered all night broke like a wave, and they followed it willingly into the darkness.

Outside, the faint noise of late-night trick-or-treaters or party stragglers drifted through the quiet neighborhood. Inside, a hush settled—broken only by soft murmurs and the sound of two hearts beating in unison. She whispered his name, he whispered hers, and the door closed, leaving them in the intimate cocoon of a new chapter in their story.

MORNING LIGHT SPILLED through the bedroom curtains in gentle gold, rousing Aimee from the deepest sleep she'd had in ages. For a moment, she forgot the previous night, lulled by the soft sheets and the comforting warmth of another body beside her. Then it all came rushing back—the party, the dance, the kisses, and finally *this*.

She rolled onto her side, and there he was: Malakai, on his back, one arm draped over his stomach, the other near her pillow. His face was turned toward her, mouth parted slightly, chest rising and falling in a calm, steady rhythm. He looked so peaceful. A tender ache filled her, and she gently reached out, brushing her fingertips along the back of his hand.

At her touch, he stirred, blinking a few times before his gaze settled on hers.

"Morning," she whispered.

A lazy grin touched his mouth. "Morning," he echoed, shifting to face her. Neither spoke for a beat, basking in the quiet of a Sunday morning where no alarm demanded their attention.

Aimee's heart felt like it might burst. She couldn't recall the last time she'd let someone into this personal space—and felt so right about it. Slowly, she slid her hand into his, and he gave it a gentle squeeze.

"Any regrets?" he asked softly, eyes searching hers for uncertainty.

She swallowed, finding none. "No," she said, breath catching. "I'm… glad you're here." Relief and something warmer bloomed in her chest. They'd taken a leap, and waking up in his arms confirmed she'd land safely.

His smile was soft with relief. He leaned in to place a tender, lingering kiss on her forehead, a small gesture that brought back every flutter from the night before. "I wasn't sure how you'd feel this morning," he admitted, his voice low and cautious. "About…everything."

She freed her hand to rest it lightly on his chest, feeling the steady thump beneath. "I'm still processing it," she said, stomach fluttering at the memory of just how close they'd gotten last night. "But in a good way. It feels… right."

He hummed agreement, dipping his head for a chaste kiss on her lips. The contact sparked a fresh glow of happiness. He was here, for real, and he wanted to stay. The realization made her exhale a shaky laugh. Then her stomach rumbled, embarrassingly loud.

Malakai raised both brows, trying not to laugh. "Sounds like the chef might need breakfast," he teased.

She rolled onto her back, letting out a dramatic sigh. "I guess so. But ironically, I have *zero* energy to cook. I blame you." She shot him a playful side-glance.

"Oh, is that how it is?" He propped up on an elbow, the sheet sliding down to reveal the muscular line of his shoulder. Heat flooded her cheeks, and she swallowed, determined not to stare. "Maybe I should be the one whipping something up this morning. A small apology meal, to make up for my crimes."

Aimee bit her lip, fighting a grin. "Do you even know how to make anything besides scrambled eggs?"

His offended look was so theatrical she had to giggle. "Wow. That's how little faith you have in your star apprentice?" he quipped, then shrugged. "But… you're not exactly wrong."

She laughed softly, loving how easy it felt to banter with him —even here, in this vulnerable moment. "All right, star apprentice. You handle toast. I'll do coffee. Think you can manage that?"

He gave her a mock salute. "Yes, Chef."

They freshened up together, occasionally exchanging shy, playful glances that underscored just how new this closeness was. Once they emerged into the living room, the quiet of her home pressed around them, contrasting sharply with the vibrant party from hours ago. Aimee flicked on the kitchen light, grabbing the bag of coffee grounds while Malakai rummaged for bread.

"I've never had someone stay over before," she said, half talking to herself. Then, bracing her hands on the countertop, she turned to face him. "I usually like my space."

He set the bread aside, crossing to her, warm hands settling at her waist. "I'm glad you let me in," he murmured. Then he kissed her, softly but with a tenderness that made her toes curl.

Her heart soared, and she pushed up on her tiptoes to deepen it, if only for a moment. When they broke apart, she couldn't stop smiling. "So... coffee first, then toast. And then we'll see where the day takes us?"

His grin matched hers. "That sounds perfect," he said, eyes gleaming with possibilities that went far beyond Sunday morning.

Aimee's pulse fluttered in anticipation. Last night had changed everything between them—opening a door not just in her home, but in her heart. She had no idea where their newfound intimacy would lead, but for the first time in a long while, she was eager to find out. The morning sunlight spilled across the countertop as she measured coffee grounds, and Malakai made an exaggerated show of popping bread into the toaster.

They shared a quick, secretive laugh, the kind of moment that only two people on the brink of love understand. And as Aimee watched him fumble with the toaster, she thought that, yes, maybe letting him stay over was the best decision she'd made in a long time.

CHAPTER NINETEEN

Malakai tugged off the oven mitts and flexed his fingers. He peeked at the roast beef steaming on the dining table, its savory aroma mingling with the buttery rolls and baked vegetables Aunt Rochelle had spent the afternoon perfecting. The decorations she'd scattered—tiny pumpkins, autumn leaves, and a warm orange tablecloth—added extra flair.

He glanced back at Rochelle, who patted her apron with a hint of self-satisfaction. "You keep looking at that roast like you're responsible for its existence," she teased, arching an eyebrow. "You hang up those mitts before Aimee walks in and thinks you actually did something besides wash dishes."

"I set the table, too," Malakai countered, trying for a wounded look. He lifted the mitts as proof of his earlier duties. "And I did all that cleaning. You're welcome."

Rochelle waved her hand dismissively. "Mmm-hmm. It was barely half an hour's worth of work, baby." Her tone was playful, but she nodded in appreciation. "Though I can't lie, I'm grateful you saved me from having to scrub those bowls."

Malakai hooked the oven mitts on the side of a cabinet and

caught the scent of fresh orange juice as Rochelle poured it into a tall jug. "You really pulled out all the stops tonight," he remarked, leaning against the kitchen counter. "We've got rolls, baked beans, roasted veggies, and your crown jewel—roast beef."

A soft smile flickered across Rochelle's face. "Someone's gotta welcome Aimee properly. And I want to remind her who taught her a thing or two about cooking." She wagged a finger. "Don't let her fool you. That girl's talented, but if I didn't let her experiment with my menu, she wouldn't be half as good."

Malakai chuckled. "You do love to take credit, don't you?"

"Always," Rochelle said, placing the jug on the table. Her expression softened slightly. "But, jokes aside, I do like that girl. She's good for you."

The doorbell chimed before he could answer. Malakai flashed a quick grin at Rochelle. "I'll get it." He strode to the front, telling himself not to dwell on what she'd just said. But her approval lodged a warm feeling in his chest.

A few moments later, Aimee appeared by his side, shrugging off a light sweater. "Something smells phenomenal," she said, taking a deep breath. "Is it possible to be hungry just from standing in your doorway?"

"Very possible," he said, leading her into the dining room. "Especially when Aunt Rochelle's cooking."

Aimee's eyes landed on the spread: the glistening roast, the mashed potatoes sprinkled with parsley, and roasted carrots that looked caramelized at the edges. Her face lit. "Wow... This looks like something straight out of a holiday special on TV."

Rochelle, already pulling out a chair, motioned for them to sit. "It only looks that way because *I* made it." She spun on her heel and planted her hands on her hips, pretending to size Aimee up. "You'll have to let me know if it beats your diner creations."

Aimee laughed, sliding into her seat. "I'll try to be brutally honest, Rochelle." She pressed her hand over her heart, eyes twinkling. "I wouldn't dare sugarcoat my review."

"Good." Rochelle adjusted her oven mitt apron, glancing from one to the other. "Now that we're all cozy, let's dig in."

Malakai helped serve the first slices of roast. He caught Aimee's delighted expression as he handed her a plateful. "Careful, it's hot," he warned.

"Hot and perfect," she replied, spearing a small bite with her fork. She popped it into her mouth, moaning dramatically. "Oh, *this* is trouble. You really might be the queen of roasts, Rochelle."

"She's not bad, huh?" Malakai said, sliding into the chair next to Aimee. "I've tried to keep up, but let's be real, I can't hold a candle in the kitchen."

Rochelle pursed her lips, pointing her fork at him. "Yet you still attempt cooking lessons with Aimee. I hear there were flames involved."

Aimee snickered, scooping some gravy over her mashed potatoes. "He *insisted* he'd help me learn a new recipe. In reality, I had to shut the stove off before the whole kitchen turned into a fire pit."

Malakai's cheeks warmed. "Okay, but we agreed never to speak of that again."

"Ah, so it *was* a mini fire," Rochelle cackled. "You are *definitely* my nephew."

He groaned. "This is what I get for trusting you both. A double roast—no pun intended."

Aimee leaned over and nudged him. "We still had fun, right? Plus, you brought me a peace-offering dinner afterward, so all is forgiven."

Rochelle tapped a finger to her chin. "Speaking of forgiveness, Aimee, how long do you intend to give this big lug a chance?" There was a teasing glint in her eye. "Any future plans I should know about… like grandchildren?"

Malakai nearly sent his fork flying. "Aunt Rochelle!"

Aimee offered a mock-serious sigh. "I keep telling him he can't set the kitchen on fire if we have kids running around. So until he stops endangering my stove, we'll wait on that."

Rochelle slapped the table, laughing so hard her shoulders shook. "Now *that's* the best answer I've heard all week."

Malakai settled back, exhaling in relief that Aimee was rolling with Rochelle's blunt humor so easily. "We'll let you know when we're ready," he said, picking up his glass. "Until then, your roast is going to distract me from any baby talk."

Aimee winked. "Duly noted. I'm all about the roast right now."

For a while, the only sounds were appreciative hums and the scrape of utensils against plates. The house took on a cozy hush, broken occasionally by Rochelle's "mmm" of satisfaction or Aimee murmuring how the carrots practically melted in her mouth.

When they reached for seconds, Rochelle dabbed her napkin at her lips. "Malakai tells me you two have been trying new date ideas," she said, leaning forward. "I assume *non*-cooking ones, after that fiasco?"

Aimee nodded eagerly. "Yes, we've gone to a pumpkin festival, a couple of local events—even a silly karaoke night. Malakai's actually not bad at belting out old R&B classics."

Malakai let out a low groan, cupping his forehead. "Oh, don't remind me. My voice cracked in the middle of that Boys II Men song."

"But you recovered nicely," Aimee assured him, patting his arm. "The crowd loved us. Remember the applause?"

Rochelle's eyes sparkled. "Well, I never pegged you for a singer, nephew." She gestured broadly. "But if it keeps you from igniting stoves, then carry on."

Malakai rolled his eyes, though a grin tugged at his mouth. "Glad my 'talents' are appreciated."

Aimee nudged him again, trying to suppress a laugh. "They are. We'll have to do a repeat performance and invite Rochelle."

"Oh, I'd pay good money to see that," Rochelle declared, a mischievous glint in her eye.

The conversation drifted into tales of the diner's busiest lunch rushes, a rumor about a new bakery opening, and Rochelle's reminiscing about how Malakai used to trip over his shoelaces as a kid while carrying plates—"He broke at least five," she claimed, to Malakai's loud protest.

"That's an exaggeration," he mumbled, flushing as Aimee giggled. "It was maybe three at most."

When their plates were cleared, Rochelle let out a satisfied sigh. "Now, since you've both devoured my roast, we can move on to dessert. I made a red velvet cake this morning. A classic never disappoints." She stood, beckoning them to the kitchen counter. "Come on, it's best served fresh."

Aimee hopped up. "Ooh, I can't wait. Any chance you'll share your recipe, Rochelle? My last red velvet attempt came out pink-ish and bland."

Rochelle gave her a proud nod. "I'll consider it. But only if you promise not to overshadow my diner's eventual dessert menu."

"Now that's a fair deal," Aimee quipped, grabbing a spatula to help. "I'll swear not to steal your customers."

Malakai trailed behind them, lips quirking at their easy camaraderie. Rochelle motioned for him to hold back while she sliced the cake, carefully lifting each piece onto plates. Aimee hovered close, practically bouncing on her toes.

"How do you get it that deep red color without an artificial aftertaste?" Aimee asked, curiosity lighting her eyes.

Rochelle leaned over the counter, pointing with the edge of the knife. "It's all about balancing natural cocoa with just enough beet powder—though a tiny bit of dye doesn't hurt. And the vinegar in the batter helps the color pop, if you do it right."

Aimee's jaw dropped. "Beet powder? I never would've guessed."

"Keep that in your mental notes, girl," Rochelle teased, handing her a plate. "Now take this to Malakai so he can confirm I still reign supreme."

Malakai hid a grin as Aimee turned, offering him a slice drizzled in cream cheese frosting. She slid it in front of him with a flourish. "Your aunt demands a verdict."

"She demands a lot, doesn't she?" he said, accepting the plate. His fork sank easily into the fluffy red layers. One taste, and a wave of sweet chocolate tang filled his mouth. He let out a drawn-out "Mmm" that made both women smile.

Rochelle planted her hands on her hips. "Well?"

Malakai licked a smudge of frosting off his lip. "It's... basically perfect." He glanced from Rochelle's triumphant smile to Aimee's wide-eyed admiration. "How do you top this? I'm in awe."

Aimee shot Rochelle a mock glare. "All right, you've both officially raised the bar too high. No pressure on me for the next potluck or anything."

Rochelle's laugh was bright. "Practice makes perfect, hon. If you impress my nephew enough, he might even propose." She waggled her brows in an exaggerated way.

Malakai nearly choked on a bite. "Aunt Rochelle!" he hissed, coughing. "I think Aimee's got enough on her plate without—"

Aimee patted his back with gentle taps, half-amused, half-embarrassed herself. "We'll cross that bridge when we get there," she said lightly, tossing a playful glance at Malakai. "Or, you know, I'll reconsider if he ever tries to use my stove again."

Rochelle snorted. "Fair trade."

They spent the next few minutes enjoying their cake. Rochelle started describing an idea for a "Dessert Night" at the diner—Aimee jumped in with ways to decorate the dessert plates. Malakai mostly savored the moment: Rochelle's confident gestures, Aimee's animated expressions, and the subtle brush of Aimee's knee against his whenever she leaned in.

By the time the plates were cleaned, Rochelle leaned against the counter, arms folded, and fixed Malakai with a knowing look. "You haven't said much since we teased you about that potluck proposal."

He felt his cheeks warm again. "I'm just... content," he hedged. "This is nice. Good food, good company, no disasters."

Aimee reached for his hand under the counter, giving it a squeeze. "It is," she agreed, smiling softly at him. Then she raised her voice, turning to Rochelle. "And thank you for making me feel so welcome. Not every family dinner is this cozy."

Rochelle's expression flickered from smug to gentle. "Honey, any friend—or more than friend—of Malakai is family here." She paused, almost tenderly. "You keep him in line, and I'll keep you fed. Deal?"

Aimee grinned, bumping shoulders with Malakai. "Deal."

Malakai inhaled deeply, glancing between them. He wanted to speak up, to say how much it meant that they both got along, how happy it made him to watch them banter. Instead, he squeezed Aimee's hand in response, letting the moment speak for itself. The low lamp lighting bathed the kitchen in a golden glow, highlighting the smiles that crinkled at the corners of Rochelle's and Aimee's eyes. The warmth in the room felt almost tangible.

Rochelle pushed off from the counter and clapped her hands once. "All right, that's enough sentiment for one night. We should wrap up with a toast or something."

Aimee glanced around, spotting the orange juice pitcher. "We've got punch, or leftover OJ?"

Malakai grabbed the orange juice with a laugh. "Good enough. We can pretend it's champagne."

They poured three small glasses, Rochelle raising hers first. She cast a significant look at both of them. "Here's to good roasts, unstoppable chefs—and a certain nephew who should steer clear of any stove."

Aimee giggled, lifting her glass. "Hear, hear."

Malakai rolled his eyes, tapping his cup against theirs. "And here's to new family traditions. May we survive many more dinners together."

They downed the orange juice with mock gravity, then shared a round of laughter. The echo of it lingered in the kitchen as they began tidying up, already tossing friendly jabs back and forth about who cleaned what. Rochelle insisted Malakai do the bulk of the dishes—"as atonement for your cooking sins"—while Aimee cheerfully claimed she would "supervise."

"Great," Malakai said wryly, collecting plates. "I'm glad I'm so valued."

Aimee slid an arm around his waist, leaning her head briefly on his shoulder. "Your value is through the roof. But the dishes are all yours," she teased. "Kitchen hazard rules: if you can't cook, you clean."

Rochelle smirked. "You better keep her, boy. She's the only one who'll put up with that stovetop stunt."

Malakai smiled, a light warmth invading every corner of his chest. "I plan to," he said quietly, catching Aimee's eye. For an instant, she held his gaze with a softness that made his pulse skip.

Rochelle clapped her hands again, cutting through the moment. "All right, let's get this done so we can all put our feet up. Or maybe find that karaoke track you two were talking about."

Aimee started laughing. "Oh, no, not unless you want to hear Malakai sing off-key on a full stomach."

"Hey!" he protested. Then he relented with a grin. "Fine, fine. Let's see if I can at least redeem myself in front of my own family."

"Well," Aimee teased, leaning closer, "you can't do worse than the stove episode."

Their eyes met, and Malakai found himself chuckling, too. The playful camaraderie and Rochelle's unstoppable humor swirled around them, making everything feel free and easy. If this was what family dinners could be like—lighthearted banter, affectionate teasing, good food—Malakai wanted plenty more of them in the future.

With that thought tucked close to his heart, he stepped over to the sink, rolling up his sleeves. Aimee slid a towel in his direction, Rochelle started humming some old tune, and the night continued in the best way: together, brimming with laughter, and filled with the promise of all that lay ahead.

CHAPTER TWENTY

Aimee knotted a fresh apron around her waist and emerged from the diner's kitchen, holding two piping-hot bowls of pumpkin squash soup. Business had picked up in the late-November chill—perfect weather for soup that could warm spirits as much as bellies. She carried the bowls to a booth near the window, where an older couple waited expectantly.

"Here we go!" she announced cheerily, setting the dishes in front of them. "One for each of you, extra toasty. Let me know if you want more bread."

"Thank you, dear," said the older woman, cupping her hands around the bowl. "This smell alone is already reviving me."

Her husband nodded vigorously. "Better than the weather outside, that's for sure."

Aimee grinned. "Enjoy. I'll check back soon."

She stepped away, noticing how the diner's overhead lights glowed softly in the dreary afternoon. Through the windows, the sky hung low and gray, making everything indoors feel cozy by comparison. Over at a corner table, Malakai stood talking with two new customers, hands gesturing as he explained something—likely the specials board.

Aimee paused by the counter, letting her gaze linger on him. He wore an apron too, sleeves rolled up, that usual calm-yet-assured expression on his face. She felt a flutter in her stomach. *Why am I antsy?* she wondered. Lately, her mind had been circling some unnamed worry.

Ding! The bell at the entrance chimed, and Maia strode in, waving off the cold that clung to her coat. She spotted Aimee and made a beeline, weaving neatly around a pair of teenagers on their way out.

"Aimee!" she called, sliding onto a counter stool. "Got a second for me?"

Aimee nodded at Mary—who gave a quick thumbs-up and headed to refill coffees—then joined Maia behind the register. "Sure, what's up?" she asked, forcing a bright tone as she tucked a stray curl behind her ear.

Maia leaned forward conspiratorially. "I just wanted to confirm tonight's plan. You're still in for that double date in Atlanta, right? Alex texted me about the escape room, and it sounds epic—some Sherlock Holmes-themed puzzle." She wiggled her eyebrows. "We need all the brainpower we can get."

A quick laugh escaped Aimee. "Count me in. I mentioned it to Malakai, and he's on board." She fiddled with the pen in her apron pocket, but her eyes flickered to the door. "We'll drive up together."

"You sure you're okay?" Maia pressed, noticing Aimee's fidgeting. "Usually you'd be jumping up and down about a puzzle challenge. Or is all that city traffic messing with your vibe?"

Aimee offered a small shrug. "Maybe. Atlanta can be overwhelming. But I'm fine—just a weird day."

Maia studied her for a moment, then patted her arm. "If you need to vent, text me. I'll be around until we head out."

"Thanks, Mai," Aimee said softly, feeling a surge of gratitude for her friend's perceptiveness. "I'll be good, promise."

With a reassuring nod, Maia hopped off the stool. "Better run. I'm supposed to pick up some fancy cupcakes for tonight's drive. Hang in there!"

"Will do," Aimee promised, returning Maia's quick hug before watching her leave.

Trying to shake her unease, Aimee returned to her regular tasks, delivering an order of fries to a table of college students. But as she grabbed fresh mugs for another group, that niggling thought poked at her again: *What if Malakai decides to expand the diner beyond Sweetgum?* She shoved it aside—no time for that.

She pivoted just as Malakai appeared at her elbow. "Hey," he said in a low tone. "Looked like Maia had serious business."

Aimee mustered a half-smile. "Just finalizing tonight's double date." She glimpsed his concerned expression and tried to brush it off. "I'm okay," she added quickly. "We'll talk later."

"All right," he agreed gently, resting a warm hand on her forearm. "Just let me know if you need anything."

She gave a brief nod, appreciating his attentiveness, then spun to greet two women looking for a booth. *I'll hold it together,* she thought, *and we'll hash things out when the time's right.*

THAT EVENING, Aimee and Malakai merged into Atlanta's traffic, the city lights flickering across the windshield. Buildings soared above them, signs and ads flashing in every direction. Aimee craned her neck at one especially garish neon bar sign.

"Wow, that's... bright," she remarked, half in awe. "Is that normal?"

Malakai laughed, switching lanes with practiced ease. "Pretty normal for downtown. Big city life: loud, colorful, and slightly obnoxious." He turned down the radio volume. "Kinda fun, though, don't you think?"

"Sure," she said, though her tone wavered. She tapped the

window, as if unsettled by the swirl of headlights. "Must be a lot to get used to. You don't miss living here?"

He glanced over, eyebrows raised. "Miss it? Some aspects, sure. But I like being in Sweetgum right now. Don't get me wrong—Atlanta's great for a visit, maybe a weekend trip. But I don't mind heading home afterward."

She nodded, exhaling a tiny breath of relief. Still, the question gnawing at her refused to fade. A few minutes later, traffic thickened, forcing the car to crawl. Malakai shot her a quick sideways look.

"You've been quiet," he said. "Are you nervous about the puzzle game? Or did Maia say something to upset you earlier?"

Aimee twisted the edge of her coat sleeve, deciding she couldn't bury it any longer. "No, Maia's fine," she began, choosing her words carefully. "I guess… I've just worried you'd eventually want to move the diner somewhere bigger—like Atlanta or another city. You have so many plans, and it all happened pretty fast." She paused, face heating. "It's probably silly."

"It's not silly." Malakai gently rested a hand over hers on the center console. "I just didn't realize you felt that way."

She opened her mouth, closed it, then sighed. "Yeah, well, I kept telling myself it was no big deal. But it's been stuck in my head. You're ambitious, and I love that, but I can't help imagining you—us—getting pulled into a bigger environment. Maybe losing what we have in Sweetgum."

He gave her hand a squeeze. "I want the diner to thrive, definitely. But that doesn't mean uprooting it or me. I don't plan on leaving Sweetgum. This is home now," he explained, voice earnest. "Between Aunt Rochelle and… you, I have all the reason I need to stay put."

Her shoulders sagged in relief. She turned to meet his eyes, the tension in her chest loosening. "You really feel that way?

Because I've been half-expecting you to announce some major expansion in a big city."

Malakai's lips curved in a gentle smile. "I'm more interested in expanding our menu, not our location. Maybe we'll add a drive-through window or online orders. That's about as wild as I'll get."

A quiet laugh bubbled out of Aimee. "That's good to hear. I was half losing my mind with scenarios. I know it's only been a couple months, but it feels like we've crammed a year of changes into this short time."

Leaning in, Malakai pressed a fleeting kiss to her knuckles. "Hey, if something bugs you—even a small what-if—just tell me, okay? I don't want you dealing with doubts alone."

She brushed away the prickling at her eyes, heart warmed by his reassurance. "Thanks," she murmured, letting her fingers intertwine with his. "I'll do better at speaking up next time."

By then, traffic had crawled forward enough that Malakai needed both hands on the wheel again. They fell into an easier conversation, tossing around ideas for holiday promos at the diner. Soon, the city's neon gave way to a large, colorfully lit building trumpeting "Atlanta's Best Escape Room."

"That's our spot," Malakai announced, pulling into a parking slot. Across the lot, Maia and Alex waved from their own car.

Aimee unclicked her seat belt, adjusting her coat. "Guess we're about to see if we can solve puzzles under pressure."

Malakai grinned, turning off the engine. "If we get locked in there, I'll just blame you for distracting me."

"Distracting, huh?" She arched a brow, then leaned over to plant a soft kiss on his cheek. "That's fair."

He laughed, brushing an affectionate hand down her arm. "Ready, detective?"

She nodded, a playful glint in her eye. "Let's do this. And Malakai?" She paused, letting her voice drop. "Thank you. For clarifying... everything."

He kissed the back of her hand once more. "Anytime. Now let's go conquer a mystery."

They joined Maia and Alex by the entrance, greeting each other with animated waves. Aimee felt her shoulders relax as she locked arms with Malakai. The swirl of worries no longer pressed on her mind; their conversation had chased the doubts away.

Standing under the bright neon sign, the four of them joked about forming "Team Genius." Aimee laughed at Alex's insistence that they'd break the room's record time. With Malakai at her side—steady, supportive, and very much invested in staying in Sweetgum—Aimee stepped inside the building, eager for a fun, puzzle-filled evening and feeling lighter than she had in days.

CHAPTER TWENTY-ONE

Malakai scanned the medieval-style office, his gaze skipping over a narrow window, a tall bookshelf full of dusty tomes, a sturdy wooden desk, and a few shadowy paintings on the stone-like walls. Somewhere in this staged room, they had to find a key—and then figure out where it led. A digital timer, glowing red above the heavy wooden door, warned them they had only forty-five minutes.

"So," he murmured to the group, "we've got a lot of ground to cover."

Across the room, Maia thrust open a desk drawer, her tone edgy with excitement. "We've poked around the obvious spots," she said, her voice bright yet urgent. "Behind the bookshelf, under the doormat—nothing. We're going to run out of time!"

Alex, who had been methodically flipping through papers in the desk, looked up with a calm expression that contrasted Maia's animated gestures. "We still have forty minutes. Panicking wastes seconds. You keep checking unconventional spots; I'll keep searching the usual places."

Malakai couldn't help but appreciate how Alex grounded Maia's energy. He turned to check on Aimee, who was hunched over a row of small chairs. She was yanking cushions off them and peering underneath each seat.

"Want to stick with that plan?" he asked, moving closer. "We tackle weird hiding spots. Alex keeps on with the desk and shelves."

Aimee nodded, grin lighting her face as she tossed one cushion aside. "Sure—whatever finds this key fastest." She glanced over her shoulder at Maia. "Hey, come on, help me check under that mat one more time. Could be so obvious it's *actually* clever!"

Maia hurried over, shooting Aimee an appreciative grin. "We might have missed something."

Malakai tugged at his apron—he still hadn't taken it off from dinner, which he found oddly amusing. "All right, I'll try that armor in the corner," he announced, pointing to a life-sized knight statue looming behind the wooden desk.

He approached it, brushing dust off the metal joints, half-expecting a secret lever or hidden button. "They usually build more than one puzzle into these," he murmured to no one in particular. He pried the knight's metal hammer free, peeking inside the gloved palm. "Maybe this is some kind of riddle?"

The hammer rattled, revealing nothing. He replaced it with a sigh. "No dice here."

From across the room, Aimee let out a small whoop. "Maia, check behind this painting!" Malakai spun, nearly knocking into the knight's shoulder. Aimee was gesturing at a mounted canvas. "I see a gap!"

"Hold on!" Malakai called, dodging the desk and rushing to her side. Maia helped Aimee lift the painting, revealing a recessed panel in the wall. Malakai let out a low whistle. "Nice catch."

Aimee's eyes sparkled with excitement. "It's a drawer." She yanked the handle, the wood scraping softly until it popped open. "Oh, wow, it's—"

Malakai leaned in, heart beating faster in anticipation. *Could this be the key?* But the drawer held only a Rubik's Cube, heavier-looking than usual. Aimee gingerly held it up, rotating it in her hands.

"A puzzle within a puzzle," Malakai muttered, glancing at Alex. "Any experts here?"

Maia nudged Alex aside, taking the cube from Aimee. "Let me try. I'm not *great* at these, but I know the basics."

Malakai watched Aimee bounce on her toes, clearly itching to try it herself. He felt his chest warm at her unbridled enthusiasm. *It's nice to see her this lighthearted,* he thought. The last few days, she'd been on edge, but now her expression overflowed with focus and determination—as if no overshadowing worries existed here in the puzzle room.

Minutes trickled by—ten, maybe more—as Maia twisted and turned the cube with increasingly frantic motions. "Got it!" she shouted at last, aligning all the colors in one final swivel. The Rubik's Cube made a sharp *click*, and a metallic clang reverberated in the room.

Aimee whipped around, her ponytail bouncing. "Where did that come from?"

Behind them, the knight's armor abruptly jerked, its arm snapping upward with a metallic creak. Aimee let out a startled yelp, stumbling backward. Malakai caught her, quickly wrapping an arm around her waist for support.

"Easy," he teased, squeezing her gently. "It's just a little animatronic trick."

She exhaled a breathy laugh, leaning into his side. "Jeez, they're committed to the theme here."

The knight remained frozen, its finger pointing toward a tall bookshelf behind the desk. At once, Alex and Malakai crossed the room, stepping around the chairs. The shelf was stuffed with old tomes. Dust motes danced in the overhead light as

Malakai dragged a wooden stool closer. He climbed up, shifting figurines aside.

"Something's jingling in this one," he said, shaking a cherub statue. A dull *clank* sounded inside it.

Aimee hopped up to steady his elbow. "Careful. Don't fall."

"Thanks," he murmured, shooting her a quick, grateful grin. He stepped down, statue in hand, raising it to the lamp. No hinges or openings. "Guess we're supposed to break it," he deduced, grimacing at the cherub's innocent expression.

"I'll do the honors," Alex offered with stoic practicality. "Hand me the hammer."

Aimee's brow furrowed, but Maia gave a resolute nod. "We have to do it. Time's ticking."

Malakai fetched the knight's hammer and passed it to Alex, who tapped the cherub gently. A hairline crack formed. He gave it a few more careful whacks until the ceramic split, revealing a small metal key that tumbled out onto the carpet with a *tink*.

"Yes!" Aimee cheered, scooping it up. "We've got our key." The clock overhead read just under ten minutes. "Let's go!"

Malakai reached the door in a few strides, fumbling the key into the lock. Everyone crowded around, excitement buzzing in the air. At first, it resisted, but then it turned with a *click*, and the heavy door swung outward.

Cheers erupted from the employees waiting in the hallway. The escape room staff clapped, congratulating them on making it out before time ran out. Malakai grinned, swept up in the rush of victory. Aimee practically launched herself at him, arms sliding around his neck as she planted a quick, celebratory kiss on his lips.

"Hah!" she breathed against his mouth, her own laugh brimming with delight. He kissed her back, heart thudding from the combined adrenaline of puzzle-solving and the warmth of her closeness.

"Victory smooch," Maia joked, brushing past with a beaming

smile. She nudged Alex. "Hey, do we get a congratulatory kiss, too, or just a fist bump?"

Alex chuckled, leaning in to give Maia a quick peck. "That works, right?"

She wiggled her eyebrows. "Definitely."

The four of them strolled into the lobby, coats and purses retrieved from lockers. The staff took a group photo, capturing their triumphant smiles. As they stepped outside into the crisp night air, Maia let out a big sigh. "That was *awesome*! Who's in for ice cream?"

"Always," Aimee chimed, leaning her head briefly on Malakai's shoulder. He squeezed her side affectionately.

"Count me in," he agreed. "Perfect way to celebrate."

Alex pulled up directions to a late-night ice cream spot. As they wandered through the parking lot, Malakai draped his arm over Aimee's shoulders. The city lights reflected off the windshields around them, giving the moment a festive glow. He caught the teasing sparkle in Aimee's eye and felt a surge of contentment.

Yes, he thought, guiding her toward their car, *sometimes it's nice to leave serious worries behind.* The puzzle game had reminded him how good it felt to share easy, playful moments with Aimee—no tension, just laughter and camaraderie.

MALAKAI PULLED up in front of Aimee's small house, headlights illuminating the snow-dusted porch. Soft flurries drifted under the streetlamp, giving the entire neighborhood a gentle, wintry hush. He shifted the car into park, letting the engine idle. Aimee unfastened her seat belt and turned to him with a little smile. The overhead light caught faint crystals of melting snow in her hair.

"Thanks for driving," she said, voice low with lingering

contentment. "I didn't realize how tired I'd be after all that excitement."

He twisted in his seat, returning her warm look. "Anything for you," he teased gently, eyes flicking to her lips before meeting her gaze again. *It's never enough time,* he thought. They'd spent hours together in the city, yet he still didn't want the night to end.

Aimee parted her lips, as if to say something else, then hesitated. "You want to come up on the porch?" she asked, a shy tilt in her tone. "I—I mean, just to make sure I get inside okay."

A slow grin spread on Malakai's face. "Sure," he murmured, turning off the engine. "Gotta protect you from any dangerous snowflakes."

She laughed softly, slipping out of the car. The night air bit at their cheeks, but neither of them rushed. He joined her on the sidewalk, snow crunching lightly underfoot. She shivered once, and he tugged her close, guiding her up the short path to the porch step.

The soft glow from her porch light cast them in a warm circle. Aimee turned to face him, cheeks flushed—not just from the cold. "So," she said softly, biting her lip in a way that tightened his chest. "That escape room... we make a good team, huh?"

He set a hand on her waist, letting out a contented sigh. "We do. Maybe we should solve mysteries together for a living," he teased. "Quit the diner, start a detective agency—'Aimee & Malakai, Puzzle Experts.'"

She giggled, leaning into him. "Tempting, but the diner needs us more." Her eyes flickered with gentle affection. "I'm just glad we got to unwind. It's been a weird few weeks, with me overthinking everything."

His arm curled more firmly around her. "And me not seeing it. I'm sorry if I missed the signals, Aims."

Her face softened. "No need to apologize. You've been amazing… truly. I just had to figure out how to talk about it." She let out a quiet laugh. "Now I feel silly for worrying so much."

He dipped his head closer, brushing his lips against her temple. "Don't feel silly. Sharing doubts is hard." He swallowed, his heart thumping with the desire to tell her more—to say the words that had been building for days, maybe weeks.

Aimee noticed a shift in his mood. "Hey," she whispered, studying his face. "You okay?"

He drew a slow breath, exhaling a puff of steam into the cold air. "Yeah. Just… I care about you. A lot. More than I thought possible."

Her eyes rounded slightly, hope shining there. "I care about you too," she said, voice trembling with feeling. "I—I'm so glad you ended up in Sweetgum again."

Something in Malakai's chest tightened. *Is this the moment?* He found himself cupping her cheek, thumb brushing lightly across her chilled skin. "Aimee," he began, heart hammering. "I'm— I'm in love with you."

She froze, lips parting. Snowflakes drifted between them, silent witnesses to the confession. Then her expression lit with a radiant warmth that sent Malakai's pulse soaring.

"You really mean that?" she breathed, voice wavering. A thousand emotions danced in her eyes—surprise, relief, overwhelming joy.

He nodded, leaning his forehead against hers. "I've never been surer. You… you make me feel like I'm exactly where I need to be."

A beat of silence, then Aimee's arms encircled his neck, and she let out a shaky laugh. "I love you, too," she whispered, as if she could hardly believe the words herself. "I've been wanting to say it… thought maybe I'd blurt it out at a random time, but this is better."

Malakai let out a breath he hadn't known he was holding, euphoria bursting in his chest. He cradled her against him, pressing a gentle, lingering kiss to her lips. Every brush of contact felt electric, the cold air intensifying the heat between them.

When they pulled back, a wry smile danced on Aimee's face. "I guess that means there's no more reason to hold back now, huh?"

He smiled—soft and sure. "None," he said quietly, lifting her hand and pressing a tender kiss to her knuckles. "I don't want to hide a thing."

Aimee's cheeks burned pink, and her eyes brimmed with unspoken delight. "Want to come inside?" she asked, tugging his hand toward the door. "We can warm up with some hot cocoa."

A low hum of anticipation fluttered through him. "I'd love that." He let her guide him forward, stepping onto the porch proper. Before she turned the key, he squeezed her hand once more, needing to feel the solid, reassuring reality of her warmth.

"Thank you for tonight," she whispered, leaning against the door. "For everything, really."

Malakai dipped his head, meeting her gaze. "No," he said, voice gentle. "Thank *you*." He sealed the sentiment with one more soft kiss.

The lock clicked, and they slipped into the quiet of her house, leaving the snow-dusted world outside. With the door shutting behind them, Malakai felt a hush of contentment settle in his chest. The words were said. *I love you*—simple, powerful, and exactly what he needed to share. And now, as they shed coats and boots, he couldn't contain the smile that lingered, or the warmth that bloomed every time Aimee's eyes found his.

CHAPTER TWENTY-TWO

Malakai eased the oversized, cartoonish hot-chocolate cutout against the diner window and stepped back, squinting to check it was level. Twinkle lights wrapped the window frames, and miniature snowmen perched along the counter—clear signs that the holidays had arrived in full force. Behind him, someone snapped a cellphone photo, prompting him to strike a mock-heroic pose.

"Looking good, boss," teased Marsha, one of the cooks. She tugged on the cutout's corner to secure it with tape. "Kids'll love this."

Malakai nodded, taking a sip of the steaming cocoa in his other hand. A delicate aroma of vanilla swirled up—one of Aimee's special seasonal recipes. "They'll go nuts for it," he agreed, stepping away so another staff member could add tape. The sweet rush of cocoa warmed him more than the overhead heater. *Everything's coming together*, he thought. "Thanks for the help, Marsha."

She smiled. "Anytime. Mind if I grab a photo for the diner's social page?"

"Go for it." Malakai stepped aside, letting her capture the

shot. At this late hour, only two customers remained in a corner booth. They were new travelers who'd dropped in after hearing about the diner's "incredible winter menu." That particular phrase—incredible winter menu—still made him glow with pride. "That's exactly what we aimed for," he murmured, half to himself. Aimee's magic in the kitchen had drawn them here. The success belonged to her just as much as it did to him.

He wandered behind the counter, humming a muffled Christmas tune under his breath, mind drifting to the previous weekend he'd spent with Aimee—how natural it felt waking up to her. And then a far bigger thought tugged at him: *Is it too early to propose?*

He shook off the question, sipping more cocoa.

Suddenly, the bell over the door jingled, and Aunt Rochelle swept inside, her arms raised like a pageant winner. Half the staff erupted into cheers. It had become a tradition to greet her with applause whenever she popped by in "retirement mode."

She eyed the hot-chocolate cutout with a wry grin. "Well, look at that—did y'all hire a new mascot?" she teased. "All these fancy promotional gimmicks, pulling in the crowds, huh?"

Malakai planted one elbow on the counter and gave her an exaggerated shrug. "Gotta do something to stand out in December," he replied with a playful grin. "Besides, a big cartoon mug is hard to ignore."

"Mm-hmm." Rochelle peeled off her coat and folded it over her arm. A subtle floral perfume clung to her sweater, which was a sleek, deep-blue turtleneck—more stylish than her usual attire. "You're turning this diner into a city-slick operation, you know," she joked, wagging a finger. "Next thing, you'll be handing out flyers at the doorstep."

He feigned scandal. "Oh, I'd never stoop to flyers," he said, tapping the side of his cocoa cup with a smirk. "But a giant mug with a smiling marshmallow face? That's just marketing gold."

She rolled her eyes. "Still my diner at heart, I hope?" A note of genuine affection threaded her voice.

"Always," Malakai assured her. Then he nodded at her sweater. "Look at you, all fancy. Dare I ask where you've been?"

Rochelle pursed her lips. "A lady can look good just for herself, can't she?" She swatted at his shoulder lightly.

He laughed, raising his hands in surrender. "I'm not judging, Aunt Rochelle. Just noticing. You normally wear cozier sweaters, that's all."

She planted her fists on her hips, but a flicker of amusement glinted in her eyes. "Never mind my wardrobe choices. What about Aimee? I hear she clocked out early today. And since I won't get a chance to grill her, guess I'll grill you instead."

Malakai set his cocoa aside, posture relaxing. "We're great. Actually…" He lowered his voice, glancing at the staff tidying up behind the counter. "We said 'I love you' last week," he confided, letting the pride in his tone slip out.

Rochelle gave a sudden whoop, startling the waitress nearest the register. A few curious eyes darted their way. Malakai waved them off, cheeks warming as he hissed under his breath, "Keep it down."

"Oh, hush," Rochelle said, her glee shining. "You two are in love. Why not shout it from the rooftops? I bet half the folks here already guessed."

He rubbed the back of his neck, chuckling self-consciously. "It's new, that's all. But yeah… we're serious. She's… I mean, if you want to talk about wife material," he admitted, voice rising with genuine passion, "she's it. Kind, insanely talented, patient —" He caught himself when one of the waitresses made a soft, dreamy sound. He cleared his throat. "I sound like I'm gushing."

Rochelle's grin turned mischievous. "Because you are. So, wedding bells soon or what?"

Malakai coughed, nearly choking on air. "That's… not the

next immediate step," he stammered. "We literally just said 'I love you.' I don't want to freak her out by proposing tomorrow."

One of the servers, leaning on the counter, chimed in with a thoughtful shrug. "If it feels right, it feels right. There's no rule on timing, boss."

"See?" Rochelle nodded, hooking an arm around Malakai's shoulders in a half-hug. "I taught him well, but he's a cautious boy."

Malakai's cheeks burned with a mix of amusement and mild embarrassment. "I'll think about it," he conceded, "but no promises. I want it to be perfect. Maybe… maybe after the holidays?" The quiet confession hung between them.

Rochelle patted him gently. "Whenever you do, baby, I'll be right here waiting to cheer—nice and loud," she teased. "Now, how about you treat me to a cup of that cocoa?"

He laughed, relieved for the shift in conversation. "Your wish is my command, Auntie."

～

THE FOLLOWING AFTERNOON, Malakai strolled down Main Street with Alex. They passed holiday-decorated windows, garlands draped across streetlamps, and a few kids bundled up in bright coats. Malakai tugged his gloves on tighter, the cold seeping through his jacket sleeves.

"So," he said, glancing sidelong at Alex, "I cornered you for lunch partly because I need a guy's perspective. I, uh… might propose to Aimee soon. Or, at least I'm thinking about it."

Alex's eyes widened fractionally before settling into a calm, approving smile. "Sounds like you've reached that point. Congrats, man. But you don't look entirely sure?"

Malakai blew out a breath, a small cloud forming in the chilly air. "I'm sure I love her—more than sure. But we've only been official a few months. She did mention everything's moving fast."

Alex nodded, adjusting the collar on his coat. "Everyone's timeline is different. Maia and I waited ages—back and forth, you know how that went. But I've seen couples who knew within weeks. If Aimee's told you she loves you, too, it sounds like you're on strong ground."

"You think I should just talk to her about it first? No big surprise?"

"Up to you," Alex replied with a small shrug. "Some people love the surprise gesture. Others prefer to know the conversation's coming. You know Aimee best."

Malakai chewed on that. "Yeah. We're planning to spend the holiday together. Maybe I'll see how she's feeling about the future in general—drop a few hints?"

"Good plan," Alex agreed, biting into a hot dog he'd just bought from a street vendor. "That's how Maia and I tested the waters. Didn't want it to be out of left field."

A comfortable silence settled between them. Malakai noticed the twinkling Christmas lights overhead, a half-finished garland flapping in the breeze. A swirl of excitement rose in his chest, imagining the possibility of Aimee in a beautiful white dress, or them exchanging vows in front of Aunt Rochelle and their friends. It made him grin like an idiot.

"So, you're good?" Alex asked, spotting Malakai's expression.

Malakai chuckled. "Yeah. I'm... more than good. Thanks, man."

MALAKAI PUSHED OPEN the office door, half expecting an empty room. Instead, he found Aimee perched on the edge of his desk, a stack of folders in her lap. She'd changed out of her uniform into a snug, cable-knit sweater, her hair loosely pinned back. His heart did a little flip at the sight.

She looked up, brightening immediately. "Hey, you," she said. "I was organizing receipts while it's quiet. Hope you don't mind."

He shut the door, crossing to her with an affectionate grin. "I don't mind at all, Ms. Overachiever. If you keep this up, you'll be doing my entire job soon."

Her cheeks curved into a playful smile. "Watch out, or I might." She set the folders aside. "Did you see our holiday sales numbers? We're drawing more visitors than ever—there's even talk of local shops thanking *us* for the extra foot traffic."

His chest swelled with pride. "That's amazing. But it's mostly your cooking that's winning hearts, not my cardboard cutouts."

She laughed, kicking her feet gently. "You're the one who put them up, though." Then she paused, eyes sparkling. "So I guess we're a pretty good team."

He stepped closer, bracketing her hips with his hands. "Definitely," he murmured. In the overhead light, her eyes shone with warmth, and the subtle fragrance of her hair—faintly vanilla—drifted up, pulling him in. "Speaking of team, how about we plan a Christmas date night soon? You know, just the two of us… Maybe dinner at my place?"

Aimee's face lit up. "I'd love that. Especially if we can wrap presents together. I have a sneaking suspicion you need help picking Aunt Rochelle's gift." Her tone turned teasing, but gently so.

He rolled his eyes with good humor. "You're not wrong. Last time, I got her a scarf that mysteriously vanished two weeks later."

She giggled, threading her arms around his neck. "Don't worry, I'll guide you." Then her voice dropped, a private excitement flickering. "And just so you know, I've been working on *your* present. I can't wait to see your reaction."

His heart fluttered, reminded of the ring question. But he forced himself to play it cool. "Now I'm all curious," he said, leaning in to brush a soft kiss at the corner of her mouth. "Maybe I'll have to outdo you."

She smacked his chest lightly, eyes dancing. "Always competitive," she teased, before slipping her hands over his shoulders to pull him in for a deeper kiss.

His breath caught as her lips parted gently against his. He found himself melting into that warmth, arms circling her waist until she was snug against him. When they finally eased apart, she exhaled, a rosy tint coloring her cheeks.

"Thanks," she whispered. "For, well… everything. It's been a whirlwind year, but you make it all feel right."

He swallowed the sudden knot of emotion. "Aimee… you've done the same for me," he said quietly, leaning his forehead against hers. Her presence was a gentle anchor, making him forget any anxieties about the future.

She smiled, relaxing into his arms. "So, Christmas is around the corner. Hope you're ready for some 'couple traditions.' I'm big on decorating gingerbread houses."

Malakai chuckled softly. "Bring it on. I'll probably burn the icing somehow, but I'm in."

"You'd better not," she joked, a delighted gleam in her eyes. Then, calmer, she murmured, "I can't wait."

They stood like that for a moment, the faint hum of the diner's air conditioning underlining their cozy hush. The unspoken promise hummed between them—that this Christmas might be the start of something even more permanent.

Finally, Aimee disentangled herself, cheeks still flushed. "You're closing up soon, right? Let's finish these last tasks so we can get out of here."

He pressed a last soft kiss to her temple. "Right. Lead the way, Ms. Organized." Her laughter brightened the office as she slipped from his hold, grabbing the folders again with deter-mined efficiency.

Malakai watched her, affection brimming in his chest. *Yes,* he thought, *Christmas might be the perfect time.* He just needed a bit more courage—and maybe a ring that said forever.

EPILOGUE

$\mathcal{M}$alakai hummed softly to himself as he paced down the hallway of Aimee's home, double-checking every surface for stray belongings. Just outside, through the window, he could see Maia's car pulled up at the curb, trunk popped open as she carefully stacked plastic containers of holiday goodies. *We're running late*, he noted, his stomach dipping with a small bolt of nerves. But it was Christmas Eve, after all, and a bit of organized chaos felt almost fitting.

Pausing by the living-room table, he made sure no trays lay forgotten behind the throw pillows. His gaze drifted over the soft glow of Christmas lights that Aimee had wrapped around a nearby shelf—a last-minute decoration spree they'd done while sipping eggnog a few nights ago. Even in the mild mess of final prep, her home felt cozy, welcoming.

If all went well, by the end of tonight, she'd be his fiancée.

He followed the clank of dishes to the kitchen. Aimee was there, hurrying between counters with an almost frantic speed. Plastic wrap, greased parchment, and the aroma of freshly fried chicken filled the air.

"Everyone else is already at the diner," Maia said, bustling in with a box of Christmas-themed brownies and sliding them onto the counter. "We're easily half an hour late. They're probably hoarding the appetizers, and soon they'll have nothing else to eat." She shot Aimee a pointed grin, then aimed a playful wave at Malakai over her shoulder.

Malakai's lips twitched at how seamlessly Maia teased Aimee about *him*. He stepped over to offer Aimee a fresh roll of plastic wrap. "We'd better pick up the pace," he said lightly, though his own excitement fluttered inside him. "I promise not to blame you if they start devouring napkins from hunger."

Aimee snorted a laugh, securing the last tray of chicken legs with the wrap. "Don't even joke," she said, flicking a glance his way. "Are you upset at me for taking so long?"

He leaned in a fraction, lowering his voice so only she could hear above Maia's rummaging. "I'm never upset at you," he said gently. "But I *am* eager to get there. Everyone's waiting—and we can't starve them on Christmas Eve."

She exhaled a small, relieved sigh. "Right." Her phone buzzed on the counter, and she glanced at the screen. Malakai caught sight of the text message:

Mary: Everyone's loving the appetizers.

Attached was a photo of Sean from the local dance studio, spinning a woman near the diner's front counter. He saw Aimee's face warm with delight.

"Aww," she murmured, eyes bright with affection.

"Sweet," Maia said, whisking a final box out the kitchen door. "Now if you two lovebirds are done gawking, let's move!" She called out from down the hallway, voice echoing as she headed outside.

Aimee set her phone aside, pulling off her apron and letting Malakai grab the last sealed tray from the counter. Together, they followed Maia onto the porch, where the trunk of her car yawned open under flickering holiday lights. The neighborhood street was a serene swirl of colorful displays, each house shimmering with Christmas spirit.

Malakai placed the tray in the trunk, stepping back. Aimee slid into the passenger seat, boxes cradled on her lap. "You driving alone?" she asked through the open window, a small furrow of concern knitting her brows.

He offered a quick, reassuring smile. "Yeah, I parked down the block. I'll see you at the diner in a few minutes." Then he dropped his voice conspiratorially: "I have to check on something first—last-minute errands. Don't worry."

Aimee narrowed her eyes, but a fond spark danced there. "Fine, Mr. Mysterious. Just don't keep us waiting forever."

Malakai tapped the door with two fingers and accepted the quick air-kiss she blew him. Inwardly, his pulse raced with anticipation. *Tonight's the night.* If everything lined up, he'd slip into the diner just ahead of them and finalize the perfect moment.

WHEN AIMEE and Maia finally walked through the diner doors, laden with foil trays and boxes of desserts, the celebration was already roaring. Twinkle lights draped every window; the Christmas tree in the corner blinked cheerfully; and a swirl of laughter, music, and delicious aromas permeated the air.

"About time!" someone teased, raising a half-eaten candy cane in greeting. A small wave of applause followed, and more than a few playful whistles.

Aimee lifted her trays in mock apology, cheeks flushing at the sudden spotlight. "Yes, yes, we're late. But we brought extra goodies, so you'll forgive us, right?"

Nevaeh perched on a barstool near the counter, raising a gingerbread cookie. "If those are your famous chicken legs, we'll definitely forgive you," she teased, popping a bite into her mouth.

Malakai let the door close behind Aimee, stepping forward to press a warm, fleeting kiss to her cheek. "Glad you made it," he murmured, letting her feel just a hint of his excitement.

She noticed the glint in his eyes, returning the quick hug. "You didn't text me that you'd be here first," she said softly, eyebrows lifting.

He shrugged, feigning innocence. "We're on the clock, remember? No time to waste."

Before she could prod further, Rochelle bustled forward, sporting a Santa-hat headband, and promptly steered Aimee toward the back to deposit the trays. **Perfect distraction**, Malakai thought with satisfaction, turning to greet the next wave of guests.

Every corner of the diner hummed with holiday cheer. People danced near the jukebox, passing cups of hot cocoa and indulging in homemade cookies from Rochelle's stash. A handful of kids squealed in the corner booth, playing some improvised game with candy canes. The local sense of community, the swirl of red-and-green sweaters, it all set a perfect stage for what Malakai had planned.

He caught a glimpse of Aimee emerging from behind the counter, beckoned by a friend who wanted her to try some spiced cider. Each time their eyes met across the crowd, his heart beat faster. Soon, soon, he promised himself.

THE EVENING SOARED. After the meal portion, the guests dragged Malakai and Aimee into a series of silly games: a candy cane relay, a "Name That Christmas Carol" quiz, and a spontaneous dance-off sparked by Sean's hilarious breakdance moves.

Aimee laughed so hard she nearly doubled over, and Malakai couldn't tear his eyes away from her radiant expression.

"This is insane," she gasped between giggles, clutching Malakai's arm. "I love it."

He squeezed her hand in response. "Let's keep the fun going," he said, leading her into another twirl. She squeaked in mock protest but grinned widely, letting him spin her under the festive lights.

The hours rushed by in a blur of conversation, dancing, and gift exchanges. Maia gave a heartfelt toast about community, Rochelle teased Malakai mercilessly about "getting serious" in a big crowd, and at one point, Brandi demanded everyone take a group photo under the giant Christmas tree near the corner. Malakai pulled Aimee into his side for the picture, heart thrumming with the knowledge that soon, their next photo might be an engagement announcement.

Finally, as the party began winding down, some folks started drifting out into the snowy night, arms brimming with leftover treats. A hush of satisfaction fell over the diner, guests lingering in small pockets around the tree or near the hot-chocolate station.

Malakai inhaled deeply, sliding a hand over the small box hidden in his jacket pocket. *Time.*

He scanned the room. Aimee stood by the door, bidding goodbye to Maia and Alex, who had an early morning drive planned. As the door swung shut behind them, the diner was left with only a handful of staffers cleaning up and a few stragglers chatting softly in the booths.

Aimee turned back into the main area, releasing a contented sigh. "Wow," she breathed, gaze taking in the warm, twinkling tree lights. "I think we pulled off the best Christmas party Sweetgum's ever seen."

Malakai crossed toward her, hearing the crunch of stray wrapping paper underfoot. "I agree," he said, voice quiet with a new intensity. He slipped an arm around her waist, guiding her gently away from the booths and closer to the still-lit Christmas tree in the corner. "Hey, come here a sec," he murmured.

She tilted her head, curiosity tugging at her features. "What's up?"

He parted his lips, a wave of tenderness washing over him. "I was just thinking… about this place. The diner. How everything changed for me the day I walked in and saw you being so… you."

Her expression softened. "This diner changed my life, too. Meeting you here, cooking, building a community—I never expected it to lead to, well…" She trailed off, her cheeks flushing with happy color.

He swallowed, letting his thumb brush along her hand. "I never expected to fall so hard, so fast. But the more time we spend together, the more it feels like—" He paused, heartbeat hammering as he reached into his jacket pocket. "—like we're meant to build a future together."

Her gaze darted to the small, velvet box he drew out. Instantly, her breath caught, eyes flying to his face. "Malakai…"

Slowly, he lowered to one knee, the lights from the tree haloing him in soft color. The hush in the diner was absolute—whoever lingered was now silently, respectfully watching. Aimee's hands flew to her mouth, tears already trembling in her eyes.

"Aimee," he said gently, voice thick with emotion, "you took my breath away from the moment I tasted your cooking—and then you stole my heart with every conversation, every shared laugh, every hope we confided. I can't imagine a life without your warmth, your passion, your unwavering support." He lifted the ring, the diamond catching the tree's lights in tiny rainbows. "Will you marry me? Will you let me spend every Christmas—and every day—by your side?"

Tears slipped down Aimee's cheeks, her lips trembling into a beaming smile. For a heartbeat, she just stared, heart in her eyes. Then, with a soft sob that turned into laughter, she nodded frantically. "Yes," she whispered, voice shaking. "Yes, Malakai—I'll marry you."

A roar of joy went up from Rochelle, who had quietly appeared behind the counter, and any staff left in the diner broke into applause. A few tears glimmered in onlookers' eyes too. Malakai slid the ring onto her finger, his own hands shaking, then straightened and drew her into his arms. She kissed him fervently, her tears mingling with laughter, an overwhelming rush of relief and joy flooding them both.

When they pulled apart, breathless, Aimee brushed a hand across her damp cheek. "I—I can't believe it," she said, staring down at the ring. "It's… perfect."

He cradled her face, pressing his forehead gently to hers. "You're perfect," he whispered back, still dazzled by the swirl of sensations. "Merry Christmas, my love."

She let out a delighted, tearful giggle. "Definitely the best Christmas ever," she agreed, voice catching on emotion. Then she leaned in for another soft, lingering kiss that seemed to seal the promise that, from this day forward, they belonged together.

In the afterglow, the few staffers and neighbors who remained rushed in for hugs, Rochelle near the front with shining eyes. Christmas carols played softly in the background, but to Malakai, it felt like the world had gone still, anchoring around just him and Aimee, her ring flashing in the festive lights.

"I'm so happy for you two," Rochelle exclaimed, swiping at tears before pulling them both into a fierce hug. "Best Christmas gift I could ask for!"

Aimee pressed her face against Rochelle's shoulder, giving a watery laugh. "Thank you for everything," she whispered.

Malakai wrapped an arm around them both. "Yes—thank

you," he repeated, voice husky. The entire diner seemed to hum with warmth, the final hours of Christmas Eve bringing them all a moment of pure, incandescent joy.

Soon, the music rose again, and a new wave of laughter spread as more folks realized what happened. The diner glowed beneath the twinkling strands of lights, bearing witness to a perfect ending—and an even more beautiful beginning. Malakai and Aimee lingered in each other's arms by the tree, hearts light, imagining all the Christmases yet to come.

And in that sparkling hush, as snow drifted against the windows and the ring on Aimee's finger caught every glimmer of light, they knew for certain: they were each other's home, now and always.

AUTHOR'S NOTE

Thank you so much for reading The Harder We Fall, the ninth book in the Sweetgum Meadows Romance series of stand-alone novels. I really hope you loved it! If you enjoyed this book, please consider leaving it a review so that others may also find it. Also, if you haven't read the first seven books, yet, check them out today! Although these are stand-alone novels, the stories all intertwine and progress.

I look forward to introducing you to the other characters in this lovely, family-oriented town where each couple will find their happily ever after.

Would you like to receive bonus scenes and keep up with what's next with my upcoming books? Then, make sure you sign up for my mailing list on my website by visiting ImaniPrice.com.

ALSO BY IMANI PRICE

Book 1: Love Between Us

Book 2: Sweet Sunsets

Book 3: Infinite Kiss

Book 4: Dance With Me

Book 5: In Charge

Book 6: Forever With You

Book 7: Secret Sweethearts

Book 8: Endless Love

Book 9: The Harder We Fall

Book 10: Reservations of the Heart

Book 11: Play by Play

Book 12: Guarded Hearts

Book 13: Healing Hearts

Book 14: Dear Sweetgum

Book 15: Lanterns of the Meadows (novella)

Book 16: Drawn to You

Book 17: Under the Sweetgum Tree

Sweetgum Meadows' Visitor's Guide

To all my lovely readers,

Thank you
for
reading